FLAT TOP MOUNTAIN RANCH

The Beginning

JAMES E. DOUCETTE

Flat Top Mountain Ranch: The Beginning
By James E. Doucette © 2019

This book is a work of fiction, placed within the historical context of the American Civil War and the westward expansion of the U.S. at the expense of the Indigenous peoples who occupied their traditional lands. Descriptions of historical timelines and events may be fictionally enhanced, and the author's intent was for the actions and dialogue of known historical figures to be consistent with recorded history but may include fictional actions for the purpose of the story.

The Flat Top Mountain Ranch sign was designed, constructed, and installed by Santos Mariscal Jr. of Lockney, Texas.

Cover & Interior Design: Fusion Creative Works, fusioncw.com
Cover Photo Credit: Denise Doucette, Lockney, Texas
Back Cover Photo Credit: Victor Mosqueda, Lubbock, Texas
This interior has been designed using resources from Freepik.com

Book Production: Aloha Publishing, Eagle, Idaho, AlohaPublishing.com

Softcover ISBN: 978-1-7340498-2-4
eBook ISBN: 978-1-7340498-3-1

Available as softcover and ebook at online retailers, including Amazon.com

Published by James E. Doucette

Printed in the United States of America

This book is dedicated to Marie Doucette, my recently deceased daughter, whose talent is a beacon for our family.

Author's Note

This story is a fictional work. It includes historical figures you may recognize. Events and times described are relative and chosen to move the story along.

The protagonist, Jack Donaldson, is based on my wife's ancestor who fought in the Civil War. Her family has preserved his letters. Reading them triggered my desire to write this book. Some of his exploits are fictional, but he was wounded during the war.

Ty Jones is a fictional character. Many will recoil in horror thinking about a black man fighting for the Confederacy. It took research to find the history of the 22nd Louisiana Detachment. The black man in Louisiana fared better under Louisiana law, which was patterned after French law. There were free-born black men.

The battles that turned Jack and Ty's eyes west took place simultaneously. Jack fought at Gettysburg, Pennsylvania, and the battle ended on July 3, 1863. Ty's unit surrendered at Vicksburg, Mississippi, on July 4, 1863.

In any era, young men fight for their cause out of patriotism. I understate my thoughts about the politicians who send our young people to fight and die, but my admiration for those who fought on both sides is evident. If anyone has a problem with my position–too bad.

The period covered by this story is from 1863 to 1875.

One

Plaquemines, Louisiana – April 1861

Tiberius (Ty) Jones was born as a free black man on June 19, 1842, in Plaquemines, Louisiana. He was light skinned but would not pass for a white man. Ty stood five feet, nine inches, his physique sculpted by hard work. Hazel eyes and an engaging smile completed his chiseled good looks. He grew up on the Myrtle Grove Plantation, owned by Henri Boudreaux. The farmworkers were employees, not slaves. Mabel, the housekeeper, cared for him since birth. It was her sad job to tell Ty that his mother had died when he was born and also that his father was a white man.

As Ty grew older, he pressed Mabel to tell him who his father was. Each time, she responded, "In due time." Continued inquiry only brought a sharp rebuke: "Now hush up. I'll tell you when the time is right."

Ty's room was next to Mabel's. Each morning, she'd make sure he had a good breakfast and took him to school. He attended school with the other children living on the plantation, and the teacher was Mrs. Powell, wife of the plantation's foreman.

The plantation covered several thousand acres and bordered the Mississippi River. After school, Ty worked on the farm. Time off was spent hunting and fishing. It was an idyllic upbringing, sheltered from the horror of slavery. At night, he ate with other members of the household, and Mabel schooled him in proper table etiquette.

The city of Plaquemines, Louisiana, maintained a black militia. Ty joined two years before the Civil War started. There was no formal uniform. The only standard piece of apparel was an ammunition belt.

Word spread through the county that a Confederate major had called a muster on April 15, 1861, at 8 a.m. The men gathered at the courthouse square. The sun reflected off the statue of Andrew Jackson and his raised sword. The major's gray uniform was new, with one Silver Star on his epaulet, designating his rank, and a colorful sash around his waist held in place by a belt supporting a silver-handled sword and scabbard. A gray cowboy hat with a gold band was on his head. The major nodded to the sergeant by his side.

The enlisted man, dressed in a dull gray uniform with three chevrons on his sleeve, barked, "Attention!" Six hundred freeborn black men of the 22nd Louisiana Detachment snapped to attention.

The major jumped up on an improvised stage of cotton bales. "My name is Major Johnson. The Yankees are fixin' to invade our state. The Confederate Congress wants me to ask if you'd volunteer to fight the invaders. If you are willing, take one step forward."

In unison, the six hundred men stepped forward. Major Johnson finished, "I'll be honored to lead you." The men waved their assortment of hats and cheered.

Ty rushed home to tell Mabel. The excitement in his voice brought tears to her eyes. She screamed, "Oh, no!"

The next morning, Mr. Boudreaux entered the kitchen. "Mabel tells me you're going to fight the Yankees."

"Yes, sir."

Boudreaux shook his head. "This isn't your fight."

"Sir, I'm a freeborn man, and my unit has volunteered to fight the invaders."

"You don't know what you're talking about."

"I heard about how you went to Mexico and fought."

"That was different. You're just a boy."

"I'm almost twenty. I've got to go with my unit."

Boudreaux's face saddened. "I wish I could talk you out of this. When is your unit moving out?"

"I think in about a month."

"Make sure to stop by before you leave."

11

The unit spent the month sharpening their shooting skills, marching as a unit, and firing while standing in a formation. Major Johnson promoted several soldiers. Ty was elevated to corporal and given a squad of men to command. He proudly sewed his two chevrons on his new uniform.

The day before Ty's unit was scheduled to leave, he tapped on the library door.

Boudreaux slid open the pocket door and surveyed the young soldier. "I see they've promoted you to corporal."

Smiling, Ty responded, "Yes, sir."

Mabel entered the room. "Lordy, look at our boy." Looking at Mr. Boudreaux, she said "Don't allow him to go fight—he's only a child."

Before Boudreaux could answer, Ty spoke. "My unit is going to fight the invaders, and I'm going with them."

Dejected, Boudreaux responded, "Mabel, there's nothing I can do to stop him."

Mabel threw her arms around Ty and wailed, "Dear Lord, watch over our boy!"

Boudreaux patted his shoulder and said, "Keep your head down."

Ty turned and headed out the front door. As the door closed, he didn't see the tear running down Boudreaux's cheek. Mabel took her handkerchief and wiped it away.

Two

Vicksburg, Mississippi – June-July 1863

The 22nd Louisiana, now part of the Army of Mississippi, spent the summer of 1861 and the spring of 1862 fighting battles with the Union army led by Ulysses S. Grant. The Rebel army was slowly pushed, by an overwhelming force, into a defensive circle around Vicksburg, Mississippi.

The 22nd had fought alongside white Confederate troops and sustained over one hundred casualties. During the withdrawal to the trenches around Vicksburg, the 22nd marched through a hamlet. The gaping stares of the locals didn't bother the men, but one local ran up to Ty's squad and yelled, "You black folk caused this war. I hope y'all rot in hell!"

Ty turned to face the loudmouth, his face full of rage.

The major's horse nearly ran down Ty and the loudmouth. As he pulled up, the major yelled, "I don't see no uniform on you. These men are fighting to protect you." The major pulled his revolver and pointed it at the loudmouth. "Shut your dumb cracker mouth, or I'll blow your head off."

Trembling, the loudmouth shrank into the crowd. The major yelled at Ty, "Get back in ranks!"

Ty's unit was assigned the eastern side of the defensive trench around Vicksburg. The battle settled into a stalemate, each army taking potshots.

Major Johnson's bugler sounded assembly. "Men, you've done yourselves proud. I've just been informed that the Yankees have captured the Mississippi River from here to New Orleans. There's no way out."

The men raised their hats and in unison yelled, "Fight on."

Major Johnson stared in disbelief and raised his hand to quiet the assembled. "I am proud to be a part of the fighting 22nd."

Sleep was impossible. The sound of digging permeated the air, day and night. Trench warfare was a nasty, dirty affair, and the rains turned the trenches into pigsties. Heat and humidity fueled the fetid water at the bottom of the trench. The smell of human waste, dead bodies, and gunpowder filled the air. By the end of June, there was little fresh water and nothing to eat. The rat population in and around the besieged city disappeared—some cooked, and others eaten raw.

Major Johnson asked for volunteers to sneak through the Union lines and search for food. Ty led his patrol on scavenging expeditions. Johnson cautioned Ty, "I know you're a good squad leader. Lately, your temper is getting the best of you."

"Yes, sir. Can't explain it. I don't want to let you down."

Major Johnson was waiting as Ty's unit returned with stolen supplies. The squad leaders lined up for their unit's allocation. Johnson nodded at Ty, "You've managed to keep us alive another day. Good job."

Ty responded, "The men deserve the credit. It's getting harder to avoid the Yank patrols—they're catching on to our tricks."

"I don't think we'll be able to break out of this."

"Sir, I reckon you're right. We'll keep fighting as long as General Pemberton wants."

Ty saw the sadness on the major's face. "Probably no one will appreciate how you men have fought, but I'll never forget."

Ty thought, *Nor will I.*

On July 4, 1863, Lieutenant General John C. Pemberton surrendered his forces to Major General Ulysses S. Grant.

Major Johnson addressed what remained of the 22nd detachment. "Men, today General Pemberton surrendered. He asked me to tell you how proud he was to have served with you. The Yankee General Grant has offered to release us if we sign a statement that we promise not to take up arms against the Union. We have no choice. It's that or spend the rest of the war in a prison camp."

Before the Confederate soldiers could leave Vicksburg, they had to bury their dead. Ty and his unit dug a forty-by-ten-foot trench, six feet deep. It took three days to bury the corpses in their sector. Feral dogs and the few surviving rats feasted on the festering bodies. The men worked with grim determination.

Their macabre task completed, the 22nd marched to a large tent in the Union army's camp. A Union sergeant looked disgusted as he addressed Ty. "Make your mark here, boy, and you can go back to your master's plantation."

Ty, stone-faced, took the pen and wrote his name. "I can write, and I'm freeborn."

"Suit yourself, boy. Now git."

Three

Grahamsville, New York – April 1861

Jack Donaldson was born on July 2, 1841, the youngest of three brothers. The Donaldson family settled in Grahamsville, New York, around the 1800s. They were farmers in the spring and summer and sawmill operators in the winter. The town of Grahamsville was in Sullivan County, nestled in the Catskill Mountains, ninety miles northwest of New York City. Steep banks cut by a trout-filled stream flowed through the town. The long valley bracketed by mountains sheltered the hamlet from howling winter winds.

During a hard winter, proficiency with a rifle determined if your family had meat on the table. Hunting in the rugged terrain was Jack's favorite pastime. His keen eyesight picked out the slightest movement and animal tracks. As the youngest brother, they usually gave him the dirty work until it came time to hunt.

Each year the family looked forward to the county fair, known locally as the Little World's Fair. It was a time to meet neighbors and exchange news. The big news at the fair was the possibility of war; issues of the day seemed far away from Sullivan County.

The highlight of the fair, for the men, was a marksmanship competition. The women busied themselves, preparing for the quilt judging. First place in an event gave the victor bragging rights until next year. Jack was one of the best marksmen in the county, a title he shared with his best friends, Drew Haskill and Gene Roach.

At the shooting match, all eyes were on Jack, Drew and Gene. Eliminations resulted in the final round between the three friends. Side bets were common. Three targets, one for each finalist, were placed at fifty, one hundred, and one hundred and fifty yards. Three judges scored the event. After each round, the judges examined the targets and noted their score.

The judges stood on the bandstand next to the gazebo in the fairgrounds to announce the winners. They selected one representative to proclaim the winner. As the judge raised his hand, the crowd quieted. "The winner of this year's match is a tie between Jack and Drew. Gene will be awarded second place."

The competitors looked shocked. Jack extended his hand and whispered, "Next year."

Drew and Gene smiled. Drew commented, "Can't wait." The three competitors exchanged handshakes.

A sergeant from the Army took the stage, and a bugle sounded. The crowd stood. All attention shifted to the soldier. "Good afternoon. My name is Sergeant Harriman. I'm with the mounted rifles. It looks like the South will leave the Union. President Lincoln needs men to punish the Rebels and preserve the Union. We figure that with men who can shoot like you boys, we'll whip the Rebels and be home in time to harvest your crops."

The crowd cheered as the band struck up "Home Sweet Home." They sang in unison and ended with "I'm on my way—just set me free—home sweet home."

The sergeant raised his hands, "Okay boys, step forward and sign up to help Ole Abe save the Union."

The sergeant pointed at Gene Roach and bellowed, "You get out of line. Blacks are not allowed to serve beside white men. Army rules, not mine."

Gene Roach stepped out of line.

Jack and Drew stood in line. Drew remarked, "Gene's been our friend all our lives. He can hunt and shoot as good as us. Hell, last year he beat us both."

Jack yelled, "Why can't he join the Army?"

The potential white enlistees drifted away from the assembly.

Sergeant Harriman said, "Men, your country needs you."

Jack stopped. "Take all of us, or none—your choice."

Harriman stared, and as the crowd moved away, he shouted, "Okay. Your friend will be assigned to your outfit. I know the army's rule is stupid."

The young men lined up. Jack, Drew, and Gene were first. Broad smiles lit up their youthful faces.

Jack's father approached Drew's father, saying, "Just like us during those Indian wars."

Drew's father responded, "I know."

Four

Gettysburg, Pennsylvania – July 1863

Sullivan County's mounted rifles fought many battles leading to Gettysburg. The "two-month" war was entering its third year. Jack's unit camped ten miles north of Gettysburg and was resting up after a running fight with the Confederate Cavalry. Jack and Drew, both promoted to corporal, shared a tent. As the partners prepared to turn in, Drew commented, "We're gonna miss another harvest."

Jack smiled and said, "I expected the war to be over in two months. That sergeant never told the Rebs." Both men chuckled as they rolled over and tried to sleep.

Assembly sounded, and the troops lined up. The commanding officer, Major Horn, stood on an empty crate. "The unit's ordered to go to Gettysburg, and we've got to hold the Rebs until the infantry arrives. Break camp and mount up."

The unit was ready in thirty minutes. Horn ordered, "Forward at a canter."

As they approached a hill above Gettysburg, a runner halted the column. "Sir, General Buford sends his compliments. I've been ordered to show you your section of the ridge."

At Cemetery Ridge, Major Horn yelled, "Dismount! Horses to the rear." Each man knew his job. Three men ran to the stone wall as a fourth man led their horses away.

Jack and his squad got set up and waited. Gazing down from the ridge to a line of trees about a mile away, Jack yelled, "Here they come!"

Drew shook his head, "The Rebs are crazy to attack uphill."

With a loud yell, the Rebel troops trotted forward. Jack's company commander, Captain Kortright, sat on his horse immediately behind the men. "Hold your fire and stay down until I tell you to shoot."

The Rebels advanced in a perfect line. As the attackers crossed an invisible line, Kortright bellowed, "Let 'em have it, boys!" The sound of rifles firing in unison echoed across the ridge. Down the hill, attackers fell like dominoes.

The remaining attackers aimed and fired. Captain Kortright fell first. Jack yelled, "Drew, down!" He watched in horror as the back of his friend's head erupted in a pink mist.

Gene Roach jumped up and caught Drew before he hit the ground. Jack gasped as Gene was struck by a bullet in his chest. Their lifeless bodies fell at Jack's feet. Shaking his head, Jack assumed command of his fallen friend's squad and yelled, "Make 'em pay for it!"

The battle lasted another half hour. The Union Army's position on the hill and accurate marksmanship frustrated the Rebel attack. The Confederate troops who survived the assault stumbled over their fallen comrades as they retreated. A death-like quiet covered the battlefield. Several of the wounded could be heard calling, "Mama . . . "

That night, the Union medical orderlies removed the dead and wounded. Jack helped load the bodies of Drew, Gene, and his captain onto a wagon. As he was returning to his squad, Major Horn approached. Jack came to attention and saluted.

"At ease, Corporal. Today we beat back the Rebs, but it cost us dearly." With his eyes downcast, Jack nodded. The Major continued, "Your performance today was outstanding. The infantry is starting to arrive and will strengthen our position. I'm certain tomorrow the Rebs' attack will be better organized."

Jack motioned toward the wall. "We've begun digging in and building up the wall."

"Jack, I need to assign you the brevet rank of captain."

"Sir, I don't want to be no captain."

"I didn't ask your permission. I'm ordering you."

Jack retreated to his tent and collapsed on his bedroll. The image of his friends' deaths filled his mind. His hands shook, and he was soaked in sweat. Sleep was impossible.

Jack's unit was reinforced by infantry on the second day. This Rebel attack was better organized, but after huge losses, they retreated. On the third day, a lookout yelled, "The Rebs are coming back for more!"

Jack looked at the line of advancing Confederate troops in disbelief. His hands steadied as he surveyed the men under his command. "Okay boys, take your positions on the wall."

By the third day, the reinforced Union positions, flanked by field artillery, were ready for the Rebel onslaught. Jack commanded his troops at the wall. As the assault progressed, he was horrified at the senseless loss of life. During the battle, he was shot in his left shoulder but stayed at his post. After the battle, the company surgeon had him transferred to an army ambulance and admonished the orderlies. "This man's a hero. See that his wound is tended to."

Jack and several other wounded men climbed into a cargo wagon. They rode past the wreckage of the battlefield. All eyes focused on a hastily erected tent hospital. An orderly exited the tent. The men averted their eyes as the medical orderly threw a leg onto a pile of arms and legs. The orderly trudged back into the tent, his smock covered with blood, eyes hollow.

Major Horn visited Jack in the hospital. "We're going to make your promotion permanent."

Jack shook his head, "Sir, this war is over. I've done my time. The Rebs have lost—half of them don't even have shoes. I've had my bellyful of killing."

The major noticed Jack's trembling hands. "I just heard that the Rebs surrendered at Vicksburg, Mississippi. You're probably right, this war is almost over. After these two defeats it would be crazy for the Confederates to think they can win this war." He rubbed his chin and extended his hand. "I know how you feel, and I can't disagree with you. You're a good man, and you served the outfit well. Good luck."

"Thank you. Sir."

With his mustering-out pay, Jack purchased a 10-year-old packhorse he named Pete and a 4-year-old, sixteen-hand bay mare and named her Cutie. The horse was gentle and broken to saddle. He assembled supplies for his trip home. Jack purchased saddlebags for Pete and a western saddle for Cutie.

He needed to talk to his dad.

Five

Plaquemines, Louisiana – July 1863

Ty and several men from his unit began their trip home.

Ty's group walked south, following the Mississippi River. They encountered starving civilians and released Confederate soldiers. Several encounters almost led to violence. After the first day, they avoided the small towns and hid from other travelers.

Ty made his way to Mr. Boudreaux's home. Mabel opened the door and screamed, "Boy, you made it back! Hallelujah!" Her arms engulfed him. "My word, there's nothing to you! You're skin and bones! That uniform is nothing but dirty rags."

The library door slid open. Mr. Boudreaux's stocky frame filled the doorway. Smiling from ear to ear, with his forehead disappearing into his crown of white hair, he said, "Mabel, set another plate."

Mabel shook her head. "That boy needs a bath. I've got his old clothes hanging in his closet. I'm going to draw you a bath. Y'all talk a while."

Boudreaux motioned Ty to follow him into the library. "Take a load off your feet." Ty relaxed into an antique wing-back chair. "I heard what happened at Vicksburg. Were you there?"

"Yes, sir." Ty looked down as he answered. The library was as he remembered it, with ornate furnishings sitting on a Persian rug. The bookshelves covered one wall.

"Why are you looking down? You have no reason to be ashamed. That battle was over before it began."

Ty nodded. "Sometimes I think I was fighting on the wrong side. I knew about slavery, but I never thought about how they are treated. We had a construction battalion of slaves with our unit. Those poor devils couldn't read or write. Half of them had scars from being beaten. Their speech was foreign to me."

Boudreaux could see Ty's anger building.

Mabel's voice filled the house. "Ty."

Ty's demeanor changed as he headed for the door.

"Your bath is ready and clean clothes are on the chair. Throw those dirty clothes outside the kitchen. I'm gonna burn them."

Ty smiled and asked, "Are you going to scrub me?"

Mabel grinned and said, "If you don't get those ears clean, I'll take the scrub brush to you."

⟪·•◆•·⟫

As Ty exited the kitchen, Mabel said, "Here's a biscuit and a glass of milk, go lay down in your room until dinner."

"Yes, ma'am."

Mabel spent the afternoon preparing their meal. She tapped on Ty's door. "Dinner's ready."

Ty opened the door and rubbed his eyes. "I think I fell asleep." He followed her to the dining room.

Mr. Boudreaux was seated. "Have a seat. I've opened a bottle of wine." Without asking, he poured a glass for Ty.

Just as the men finished their first sip of wine, the kitchen door opened. Mabel carried in a tray piled high with fried chicken, fried rice, okra, and biscuits.

Mr. Boudreaux waited while Mabel took her seat. "A toast to Ty's return."

Mabel raised her water glass. "Only one drink before supper."

Ty and Boudreaux smirked but put their wine down and helped themselves to the food.

The dinner conversation was about the war and how the South did not have the resources to win the war. Mr. Boudreaux summed up the conflict as he saw it. "The South has fallen behind the North. There's an industrial revolution taking place on both sides of the Atlantic. The South is stuck in the past. The North has the majority of the manufacturing. The Confederacy has been cut in half, now that the North controls the Mississippi. This war is over, but the stiff-necked leaders in Richmond keep hoping that Lincoln will be defeated in the next election." Boudreaux pinched the bridge of his nose. "It's a shame more young people have to die."

Ty added, "Sir. I never knew how bad black folks had it. The comments and looks we got from the civilians hurt. Our fellow soldiers were at first reluctant to talk to us, but after they saw us in action, we gained acceptance." Ty became visibly angry as he told of the incident with the loudmouth. What he couldn't understand was the attitude of the Union troops after the surrender at Vicksburg. His demeanor softened as he talked about Major Johnson. "I thought all white people were like you and the Major."

"Ty, you were raised in this small community where everyone knew you. We have freeborn blacks living here. I thought slavery would eventually disappear, as it did in England. You've seen it for what it is. I tried to shelter you from that. I failed." He glanced at Mabel. "The time has come for you to know the truth."

Mabel frowned, saying, "It's about time."

Ty sat, collecting his thoughts. "I don't understand?"

Boudreaux held up his hands; his body seemed to shrink. "You know that your mama died when you were born."

"Yes, sir."

"What you don't know is that I'm your father."

Ty's face flushed as he yelled, "I . . . don't understand! Why didn't you tell me before?"

Boudreaux's eyes misted over, "I was waiting for the right time. Your mother and I shared our lives, and I dearly loved her. Before she died, I promised I'd protect you. I was waiting for the right time to tell you." He paused and glanced at his housekeeper.

Mabel gently grasped Ty's hands. "Your daddy has always loved you and protected you. Seeing you go off to war broke his heart."

Boudreaux regained his composure. "This war will set the South back for generations to come. The North is going to win, but the southern whites, even those who felt that slavery was coming to an end, will take their revenge on the blacks."

The two men sat facing each other, searching for words. Ty spoke first. "Our unit fought well. Our white officers were proud of us. Every other white person we met, either from the North or South, looked down on us. People who we were fighting to defend cursed us. The white men in the Union army insulted us even though many of the men from my unit volunteered to fight for the Union."

Boudreaux could see the anger well up again. "Ty, I tried to shelter you. Maybe I made a mistake. It bothers me to see the anger in you. You're not the bright, happy boy you used to be. For your own safety, I think it would be wise for you to leave Louisiana."

"I'm not afraid to fight."

"That's what scares me. You see what war does. It settles nothing. I fear the black people's future will be one of poverty and despair." Boudreaux's eyes scanned Ty's face. "I've thought about this and have a suggestion." He paused and looked at his son. "A friend of mine owns the King Ranch in Texas, near the Mexican border. They're more accepting of black people. He's a good man. I've written to him about you."

Ty looked around the room. "I'll miss this library. I spent many hours seeing the world through these books."

Boudreaux averted his eyes. "Your safety is paramount to me. Let's talk about this again in the morning. We'll get through this."

Mabel looked at Ty. "Help me clean up. You ain't no sergeant here."

Laughing, Ty responded, "Yes, ma'am."

Ty and his father spent the next three days planning Ty's trip. They spent their evenings discussing the uncertain future.

Boudreaux purchased a ticket for Ty on the steamer Matamoras, headed for Corpus Christi, Texas. Boudreaux bought his son several changes of clothes and gave him three hundred dollars in gold.

Six

Trip to King Ranch – July 1863

Mr. Boudreaux accompanied Ty to where the steamers docked. Traveling in the South as an unaccompanied black man was dangerous. The steamboat captain, Jesus Rios, was an old friend of Boudreaux's. At the dock, the captain greeted them. "This must be the young man we talked about."

Boudreaux put his hand on Ty's shoulder. "That it is." His eyes glistened as he said, "Son, I wish you didn't have to leave, but I know it's for the best."

Ty patted his father's hand. "I'll write as often as I can." Ty followed the captain up the gangplank. Within five minutes, all lines were cast off, and the steamer pulled away from the dock. Boudreaux stood and watched as the ship disappeared around a bend in the river.

The ship flew the Mexican flag and could pass through the Union blockade unmolested. The captain found Ty staring into the muddy water of the Mississippi. "Young man, we're living in dangerous times. To avoid trouble, I want you to work as a deckhand. My first mate knows who you are, and the rest will think you're just another deckhand. If we are boarded, just continue working." Ty was assigned to chipping and painting the upper decks. He worked alone most days and spent his nights in his cabin reading by lamplight. At meals, he sat with the crew. The conversations were about war and work.

A Union warship ordered Captain Rios to heave-to. The boarding party searched the ship, and as the crew stood in ranks, a young ensign asked each man his name and place of birth. Seamen came in all shapes and colors. The ensign approached Ty. "What's your name, boy?"

"Ty Jones."

"What is your job?"

Ty mimicked the speech pattern of the slaves. "I be painting."

"Where are you from?"

He pointed to the back of the ship. "Back yonder."

The ensign shook his head and moved to the next crewman. Captain Rios stormed down the ladder from the bridge. His Spanish accent made it difficult to understand his English. "No more. You have no right to be on my ship. We're in international waters and flying a Mexican flag."

The ensign faced the captain. "I was ordered to board your ship, and . . . "

Rios cut him off. "And inspect the cargo, not bother my crew. Your inspection is finished. Get off my ship."

The ensign's boarding party was assembled and he asked, "Chief, any war materials?"

"No, sir."

"Our work is finished here. Let's get back to our ship."

After the boarding party was underway, Ty joined the captain on the bridge. "Did I mess up?"

"You did well. The next few men in the line are deserters from the Union Army. That ensign didn't rattle you, but I was afraid the other boys would give themselves away."

The rest of the trip to Corpus was uneventful. After the ship landed and was secured, Captain Rios said to the first mate, "I'm going to escort Ty to the King Ranch headquarters at Santa Gertrudis Creek. You're in charge."

The mate extended his hand to Ty, saying with a smile, "Any time you want to sail with us again, you'd be welcome. You're a good man."

"Thank you, sir."

They arrived at the King Ranch. The main house was a two-story clapboard with a porch supporting a second-floor terrace. The view in all directions was a cactus-filled desert; sun-drenched landscape extended as far as the eye could see.

As the two men climbed the stairs to the porch, Richard King opened the front door.

Rios extended his hand, "Hola, Richard."

"Cómo estás, Jesus? Good to see you."

"This young man is Ty Jones. Henri Boudreaux asked me to introduce him to you." Rios reached into his pocket. "He gave me this letter to give you." King extended his callused hand. His lean, muscular build covered by work pants and a loose cotton shirt, boots, and spurs announced his trade: cattleman and cowboy.

King led them into the house and to his office. He sat at a cedar desk and motioned Ty and Rios to the chairs facing him. The office was decorated with cattle horns and trophies from the U.S. invasion of Monterrey—a Mexican flag, a flintlock rifle, and a plaque signed by Zachary Taylor commemorating the campaign.

King studied the letter and smiled as he looked. "I'll be happy to put you on the payroll. You'll start at the bottom and learn how to be a cowboy and run a ranch."

Work at the ranch started one hour before sunrise and lasted as long as there was light. The foreman was Gideon Lewis; everyone called him Legs. His short, sturdy trunk sat atop long legs. The joke among the cowboys was that when Gideon sat on a horse, his legs dragged on the ground. His weathered face and huge hands told of his life on horseback.

When Legs addressed the cowboys and doled out the day's assignments, each man answered, "Yes, sir."

Ty's days were spent mucking stalls, building fence, and doing whatever Legs assigned him to. He was given a green-broke 3-year-old mare and told, "Get her ready to work." Everyone was impressed by Ty's willing attitude and ready smile. The more experienced cowboys laughed as they watched him get bucked off. Ty landed and jumped up, ready to continue.

Legs walked over to the corral. "You fellas having a good time? Give Ty a hand before I put your butts on that unbroken sorrel stud."

Ty was a good student and with help from the cowboys, they wore out the mare and taught her to respond to leg cues.

By the time they were ready to brand calves, the mare was broke to ride. Legs had the other cowboys give Ty lessons on roping and dragging calves to the branding fire. His first attempt at roping failed. Legs called to him. "Get off the horse and help mug the calves."

"What?"

"Pay attention." He motioned to a mounted cowboy, "Okay, drag another calf." With the cowboy's rope secure around the animals' rear ankles, it passed between Ty and Legs. "I'll grab the rope, you grab the tail. You pull the rear end toward you." Legs lifted the rope and yanked it to his chest, flipping the calf on its side. "Jump on the rump and get your feet on the legs." Legs grabbed the front right leg and held it to the animal's body. The cowboy with the branding iron burned the hide and marked the animal for life. "Let her go!" Both men jumped up. The young cow ran out of the open gate.

Ty smiled and said, "That was fun."

Legs responded, "That it is. You'll mug and brand today. Tomorrow I expect you to do your share of the dragging. Tonight, you take your rope and horse and practice until your arm falls off."

The crew wrapped up for the day. Ty cinched up his horse and whispered, "Okay, let's practice." At dark, a weary Ty collapsed on his bunk.

Legs walked over. "Ready for tomorrow?"

"Yes . . . sir." Ty's eyes closed. Legs smiled as he walked back to his room.

Seven

King Ranch – Spring 1864

Six months passed. One morning, Ty asked, "Legs, can I talk to you?"

"Sure. Any problem?"

"No, sir, but I heard the cowboys talk about opportunities in West Texas, and I'd like to try to make my mark in this new territory before the war ends."

Legs rubbed his unshaven chin. "I can't say I blame you. A bright fella like you could go far. I'll be sorry to see you go." He paused, then added, "I'd like you to help us finish up gathering, sorting, and shipping the cattle we're gonna sell before you leave."

Ty smiled and said, "I'll do it."

Ty stayed and worked the shipping season. Mr. King stopped by the bunkhouse the day before Ty would leave. He remarked, "Legs tells me you want to try your luck in West Texas."

"Yes, sir. Someday I want my own spread."

"You've turned into a top hand, and I hate to see you leave. But I understand. I had the same desire when I sailed away from New York." King smiled. "Come outside with me."

Ty followed King outside. There was a muscled-up 3-year-old mare tied to the hitching rail. King motioned to the horse. "If you're heading west, you need a good horse."

The roan mare stood sixteen hands, with a beige mane and a spotted rump. Ty said, "I've never seen a horse with spots."

King explained, "This horse is an Appaloosa. The Nez Perce Indians breed them in the northwest. If you're heading west, you'll need a good horse; she'll carry you fifty miles before lunch."

Ty scratched his head. "I can't afford a horse like this."

"Your pa and I go back a long way. We fought together with Zack Taylor. If it weren't for him, I'd be dead. She's a gift."

The next day, Legs approached as Ty was saddling his mare, and asked, "You got enough vittles to get you to Fort Worth?"

"I figure it'll take me the better part of a week. I've got enough food for two weeks."

Legs handed Ty two pistols. "These here are six-shooters, and I want you to take a hundred rounds for reloading."

"I don't think I have enough room for all that."

Legs frowned and said, "You know that nag you broke? I'm giving her to you—I've never liked her. There are saddle-bags on her. Now get your stuff packed and be on your way."

"I don't know what to say."

"Promise me that if things don't work out, you'll come back."

"That's a promise." The men shook hands and Legs walked away.

Ty packed his equipment and headed for Fort Worth, leading the pack horse and riding his spotted mare.

Eight

Grahamsville, New York – August 1863

It was mid-August 1863 when Jack received his discharge from the army hospital. His unit had moved on. Major Horn had stabled his horse nearby. The stable manager greeted Jack. "How can I help you?"

"My name is Jack Donaldson. My company CO said he stabled my horse with you."

"He told me all about you. Your horse has been taken care of."

"Thank you." Jack saddled his horse and asked, "How much do I owe you?"

"Nothing." The manager smiled. "The saddlebag has a few days of feed for the horse."

Jack dropped his head. "I'm going home. My enlistment's up."

"You've done your part. This war needs to end."

As he rode away, he whispered to his horse, "Time to go home, Cutie."

Jack followed the back roads. The Pennsylvania country-side was taking on its fall colors. Crops lay unattended in many fields, and cattle in need of milking stood in pastures. Jack thought as he rode, *This war has gone on far too long.*

Grahamsville's main street looked deserted. The dirt road needed work. Ruts from the spring rains etched deep crevasses.

His father opened the door and greeted him. "I guess you didn't get my letter."

Jack dismounted. "I didn't receive no mail."

"Well, your mama passed away a month ago."

"What happened?" He held onto his horse in shock.

"She came down with a cold and couldn't shake it." His father paused and then said, "What are you doing home?"

"My time is up, and they discharged me."

"You can come back to work if you want—it's up to you."

Jack's relationship with his father had never been good, but this cold treatment was unexpected. Jack didn't answer him but mounted his horse and said, "I've got to see Drew's folks."

The Haskill farm was five miles outside of town. Mr. Haskill was busy in the barn and as Jack approached, he called out, "Jack, you made it back."

Jack dismounted. Mr. Haskill embraced him. "Drew mentioned you in his letters. You two always competed, but you were his best friend."

"Sir, I was with Drew when he got killed. It took me a month to get home because I was wounded."

Haskill walked toward the house and said, "Come in. His mama will want to hear this."

The kitchen was spare, consisting of a table, four chairs, a sink, and a cooking stove. Mrs. Haskill was at the stove spooning soup into a bowl. She turned and said, "Jack, you're home! Come and take a seat. It's time for lunch."

The soup was the best he'd ever tasted. As Jack explained the action leading to Drew's death, the soup's flavor disappeared. The Haskills hung on each word.

Mrs. Haskill waited for Jack to finish. "We didn't get many letters from Drew, but he mentioned how he was glad that you two served together. He didn't say much about the war, but the casualty figures in the newspapers told the story. I'm happy you made it home."

Jack looked down. "I felt I needed to see you and tell you how Drew died. He was facing the enemy when he was shot. He died quickly." Jack's eyes teared up. "I'm proud to have served with him."

After a brief silence, Mr. Haskill asked, "What's next for you?"

"I'm not certain. My mama died, and Dad acted like he didn't want to bother with me."

"It's been difficult for your dad to deal with this. When we got the news about Drew, your mom and dad were the first people through the door. Without them, we couldn't have gotten through the pain."

Mrs. Haskill's eyes filled with tears as she said, "Within a week, your mother was stricken and died. There were no doctors around. They're all off watching our children die." Mr. Haskill embraced his wife.

Jack thought, *How much more pain can I take?* He grasped his hands under the table to stop them from shaking.

Jack spent the afternoon helping Mr. Haskill with his chores. It felt right to work. That night, he tossed and turned in his friend's bed, his hands shaking uncontrollably.

The next morning, Jack and Mr. Haskill hitched up the buggy, tied Jack's horse to the back of the rig, and headed to the Donaldson farm. Jack's father came out of the house as they approached. He nodded. "Haskill."

Mr. Haskill got out of the wagon and tied the horses to the hitching rail. "Donaldson, I've known you most of my life, and you're my friend. Your son's alive and he needs you."

Donaldson responded, "It ain't right. I was supposed to die first."

Haskill's face reddened. He said, "How do you think your son feels? It's time for you to stop thinking only about yourself. My boy's dead and I can't change that. Jack's suffering. He needs his father."

Tears streamed down Jack's father's face. He embraced his son.

Mr. Haskill said, "I'm going to leave. You men need each other." He mounted his buggy and headed home.

Nine

Grahamsville, New York – Spring 1864

The sun cast a greenish glow over the valley as it sank in the western sky. Jack's brothers pulled up in a wagon, saw Jack, and jumped out. His oldest brother, Luke, grabbed him. His strong arms surrounded his little brother as he said, "By God, you're home!"

His other brother Mike beamed as he waited his turn.

Mr. Donaldson spoke, "Boys, let's cook some deer meat, potatoes, green beans, and plenty of brown gravy. We need to celebrate."

Jack added, "I'll make the biscuits."

Luke smiled. "Oh boy, now we're in trouble." The men laughed.

Jack's dad led his boys in a blessing. "Lord, thank you for bringing my boy home safe."

As they ate, Luke stated, "I'm sorry I didn't go off to war with you."

Jack smiled and said, "The army don't want no old men." Then Jack's face fell. "This war don't make no sense. I'm glad to be done with it. Enough of our friends and neighbors have died."

Jack's dad interrupted, "Let's talk about the future." He looked at Jack.

"Dad, I heard a lot of talk about the west. I'd like to see it before it's too settled."

His brothers protested. Their father raised his hand. "Jack's earned the right to go exploring."

Jack added, "Well, Mike, it looks like you'll be mucking the stables." Mike threw a roll at him.

The men chuckled. They spent the meal in friendly conversation. After eating, Jack, his brothers, and his father sat on the front porch. Mr. Donaldson spoke. "Winter's comin' on, so you'd best wait until spring to leave."

Jack nodded. "Yep."

Mike chuckled, "There's plenty of trees to cut down, boards to make, and stables to muck."

The Donaldsons cut trees and made boards throughout the winter. They had a good season. When logging season ended at the end of March 1864, the war effort consumed more lumber than could be produced, driving up prices.

At dinner in early April, Mr. Donaldson asked Jack, "You still thinkin' about headin' west?"

"Yes, sir."

"Well, we've made a lot of money this season. Your share should see you through until you're settled. If you don't find a place to your likin', come home."

Jack prepared for his journey west. He planned his route, helped by his brothers and father. Outfitting for a trip west was something Mr. Donaldson was familiar with. He'd made the trip several times as a young man. He wrote out directions, explaining as he wrote, "Take the back roads to Pittsburg. Make contact with Captain William Windsor. He owns a riverboat. His paddle wheeler makes regular trips to St. Louis."

On the day Jack was to leave, his dad said, "Your share of the farm will be waiting for you. Try to keep in touch. We'll look after the place."

Luke handed Jack a rifle. "You better have a good rifle and some ammunition."

"That's a brand-new Henry repeating rifle."

"It's a lever action and breech loading." Luke inserted rounds into the chamber. "You load it on Sunday and shoot all week. It'll hold fifteen rounds plus one in the chamber. At one hundred yards, I shot the target dead center."

Jack held the rifle. His eyes sparkled. "This is a beautiful rifle."

Luke added, "My little brother needs all the help he can get."

Jack removed his old single-shot rifle from its scabbard and handed it to Luke and inserted his new Henry.

Jack double-checked his saddle and the packhorse. "Well, I guess I'm ready." Jack embraced his brothers.

His dad gave him a deerskin bag. "There's some money for the trip. Write when you can."

His brothers and his father watched him until he was out of sight.

Jack spurred his horse. Next stop, Pittsburg.

Ten

Pittsburg, Pennsylvania – Spring 1864

Jack arrived in Pittsburg after traveling 450 miles in ten days. Cutie and his packhorse made the trip but needed rest. He located lodging and a stable near the docks.

The docks were teeming with people and stacked with supplies destined to be shipped downriver. The port was a significant hub for war materials, transportation for Union troops heading south, and Confederate prisoners heading north. The docks were at the confluence of the Monongahela, Allegheny, and Ohio rivers.

Conversations on the piers were laced with swearing emphasized with angry gestures. The smell of stagnating water and rotting food filled the air. Materials and supplies for the war effort lined the docks. Several large sternwheelers were being loaded. Prisoners under the watchful eye of soldiers lugged heavy boxes and trudged up a rickety gangplank. Jack thought, *Those prisoners are younger than me.* Their tattered uniforms hung on spare frames. *Good God, don't they feed them?* He jolted as one prisoner collapsed under the weight of his burden. A corporal yelled, "Get back on your feet, or I'll shoot you where you lie." Fortunately, another prisoner helped the stricken man to his feet and relieved him of his burden.

Jack's next encounter was with a company of young Union soldiers standing in ranks, waiting to embark on a sternwheeler. Their new uniforms and fresh faces reminded him of how his unit looked as they rode off to war. *Those boys have no idea what they're getting into. Lord, end this war*, he mused.

Jack grasped his shaking hand. He'd seen enough. Time to find his transportation downriver.

It didn't take long to find Captain Windsor and his boat. He walked aboard and asked a mate at the gangway to direct him to the captain. The mate smiled and said, "Here he comes."

Captain Windsor stood five feet, six inches. A white hat with gold trim covered his graying hair. As he approached, the mate said, "This man's looking for you."

Jack extended his hand. "Jack Donaldson from Grahamsville, New York, sir. My dad told me to find you. I'm headed for St. Louis."

At first, Windsor hesitated. Recognition brought a smile to his face as his hand engulfed Jack's. "I've known your father for a long time. I guess you have that same travel bug as he did. We'll be leaving in a week. Do you have a place to stay?" Excitement accentuated his mild English accent.

"Yes, sir. At the Seamen's Lodge. I have my horses stabled there and want to take them with me."

"We leave next Saturday at seven in the morning. Have your gear sorted out and ready to load. We stick to a tight schedule."

Lodging at the Seaman's Lodge included meals. In the roughhewn dining room, a large plank table that sat ten dominated the space. Jack selected a seat at the end of the table. He was no sooner seated when someone sat across from him. The new man extended his hand. "Good evening, lad. My name's Sean O'Brien." The stranger's Scottish accent was unmistakable.

O'Brien was a tall, muscular man with flaming red hair and a neatly trimmed beard. His blue eyes sparkled when he talked. He wore a black Stetson cowboy hat. The sweatband was brown from trail dust. He wore a pullover frontier shirt cinched at his waist with a deerskin belt and a holster containing an 1860 Colt six-shot revolver. His buckskin pants extended to his moccasin covered feet.

Jack responded, "Nice to meet you. I'm Jack Donaldson. Just arrived from home and plan to take a steamboat to St. Louis."

"You look to be military age. Why ain't you fighting?"

Jack stiffened. "I served two years and was honorably discharged. I've seen enough killin' to last a lifetime."

"Sorry, son, didn't mean to hit a sore spot. Why do you want to go to St. Louis?"

"I plan to head west. I've heard there are lots of cattle running wild, and free for the taking. Maybe I'll catch some and get into ranching."

"Laddie, you're right. Once the war is over, I suspect the trails west will be overrun. Before the fighting started, people were going to California to pan for gold. I think the new get-rich scheme will be buffalo hides."

Over dinner, O'Brien explained that he was putting together a wagon train and heading to Santa Fe, New Mexico. The journey would take eight to ten weeks and travel a well-worn trail. He'd made the journey often. O'Brien liked Jack and asked him to join the wagon train as a guide.

"Mr. O'Brien, I've never guided a wagon train. I've done a lot of tracking, and I'm a decent shot with a rifle and pistol."

"We'll be traveling with my trapping crew. Our job is to guide the train and keep it safe. A finer bunch of men you'll never meet. You'll learn a lot."

Jack looked confused. "Trapping crew?"

"Aye, we make enough money taking the wagons to Santa Fe to buy our trade goods and supplies for the winter."

At dinner the next day, O'Brien asked, "What clothes have you brought with you for the trip?"

"What I've got on plus three changes."

"Those duds won't last a week on the trail. There's a store not far from here that sells the clothes you'll need. We can go there after breakfast tomorrow."

The next day, the men walked to a store called Frontier Clothes. O'Brien commented as they entered, "Don't let the name fool you. This chap will sell you the cheapest clothes at the highest price that won't last two days."

As they entered, the proprietor greeted them. "O'Brien, nice to see you again. What are you looking for?"

O'Brien scowled. "This young man has signed on with me, and I want him to have the finest deerskin pants and moccasins you have—no funny business."

"Of course, follow me." He led them to the back of the store and measured Jack's sizes. After a few minutes, he settled on an outfit that met with O'Brien's approval. Another fifteen minutes was spent haggling over the price, with no agreement.

O'Brien bellowed as he headed for the door, "Come along, this man's a crook."

"Wait, wait . . . I'll take your last offer. You're taking food out of my mouth."

O'Brien answered, "You don't look like you've missed many meals."

With his new clothes tucked under his arm, Jack and O'Brien exited the store. "What was that all about?"

"The reason I wanted to get here early and be the first customer is that he thinks it'll jinx his day if he can't sell to his first customer."

Eleven

Trip to Missouri – June 1864

On the day of their departure, the men led their horses to the pier. A wide plank led to stalls on the lower deck. O'Brien and Jack stacked the feed they had purchased.

A mate handed each man his key. O'Brien said, "Come along. We've got to check on the oxen being loaded." The animals were being led two by two by their teamsters.

O'Brien greeted each teamster by name. The loading process lasted two hours. Captain Windsor looked over the bridge railing and yelled, "How much longer?"

O'Brien answered, "Ten minutes."

Windsor spied Jack. "Have you taken up with that bloody Scotsman?"

O'Brien retorted, "At least he'll learn how to drink real whiskey."

"Indeed." Windsor strode to the bridge and prepared to get underway.

Jack found his room and put his belongings away. The loud steam whistle announced departure. Jack made his way to the top deck. He spent the morning admiring the hills covered in spring flowers. A mate approached and told him, "The captain would like you to join him at his table tonight for dinner."

"I'd be happy to."

As the mate retreated, he said, "It's at seven sharp. Don't be late."

Jack arrived at the captain's table promptly at seven. The captain wore his dress uniform and directed Jack to the seat next to him. There were several businessmen at the table. The captain made the introductions. Windsor looked at his pocket watch as O'Brien approached. "Right on time. Five minutes late."

O'Brien responded, "If I have a choice of punishments between a cat o'nine tails and English whiskey, I'll take the whipping." The dinner guests chuckled.

"You'll never change."

"Neither will you."

Dinner was spent discussing the war. Jack sat quietly. Several men at the table glanced at Jack. Finally, O'Brien stated, "Don't keep eyeing the boy. He's done his part while you've been lining your pockets."

Windsor interjected. "I've known his family for at least thirty years. The Donaldsons are fighters. His dad spent two years on the Ohio frontier during the Indian wars. He told me his son volunteered when the war started. He's done his service, now let's discuss something else."

Jack stood. "Thank you for dinner. I'm tired." Jack thought as he exited the dining room, *Dad never told us about the Indian Wars.*

O'Brien and Windsor noticed Jack's hands shaking. Windsor whispered to O'Brien. "It took his dad twenty years to escape the demons of the Indian war."

"Aye. I'll watch over the lad."

The trip down the river was filled with minor holdups, including replacing broken paddles, stopping for wood for the boilers, and getting stuck on unexpected sand bars.

O'Brien complimented the captain on getting the boat stuck. Windsor replied, "A double serving of English whiskey tonight?" The nearby crewmen looked away, happy that O'Brien distracted the captain.

They arrived at St. Louis on schedule. Windsor kept a close watch on their progress and adjusted speed to make up lost time.

The horses and oxen were unloaded. O'Brien was greeted by members of his trapping crew. Each wore a variation of deerskin clothing and held the reins of his horse. He introduced Jack to each man. "This is Curly. Don't make any comment about his bald head. Woody here is the cook. Best to stay on his good side." The remaining men's names were Tiny, who stood six foot, four inches, Weasel, his beady eyes in constant motion, and Bigfoot.

O'Brien addressed the group. "You teamsters can ride with Woody in the wagon or walk. We'll herd the oxen to the campsite."

Twelve

Santa Fe Trail – Summer 1864

O'Brien's party arrived at the camp before sundown. Forty Conestoga wagons were formed in a circle with chains connecting each cart to its neighbor. The circle served as a corral for the livestock. One wagon tongue acted as a gate. The wagons, when loaded, each weighed eight thousand pounds. Eight well-trained, young, strong oxen were needed to pull the load of each wagon.

The crew camped outside the circle. O'Brien rode to the center of the camp, and catcalls greeted him. "'Bout time you got back."

Another man yelled, "We were getting ready to leave without you."

The men stepped down from their horses and were surrounded by men dressed in deerskin. Each man's outfit was tailored by hand. Headgear ranged from beat-up Stetsons to animal skins. All the trappers' footwear was similar: deerskin leggings and foot covers, with the soles made from buffalo hide.

O'Brien addressed the crowd. "This here is Jack Donaldson. He'll be coming to Santa Fe with us."

Jack settled into camp life, which was just like the army but neater and cleaner. These rough-looking men believed in a well-ordered camp. He was introduced to each man in the crew. Dinner that night was a tasty buffalo meat stew.

Several trappers peppered Jack with questions. "Where you from?" "Why are you headed west?" "What news of the war?"

Jack answered all the questions. When he described the battle of Gettysburg, all eyes were on him. The men shook their heads in disgust.

O'Brien held up his hand. "This lad has been through a lot. He did his time and wants to get away from war." He looked at Jack. "Come with me, lad. I have to make my evening rounds."

Jack was kept busy loading wagons. A steady stream of transport wagons arrived, filled with goods bound for Santa Fe. O'Brien assigned work and kept track of the items as they were loaded. It took nearly two weeks to complete the task.

The day of departure started one hour before sunrise. Jack helped with the oxen. Four pair of yoked oxen pulled each wagon. As each was loaded, the teamster approached the left side of the team and yelled, "Giddyup!" The teamsters guided their team into line. When all the wagons were ready, O'Brien rode to the head of the train and headed south toward Independence, Missouri, where the Santa Fe Trail began.

Jack was assigned to herd the extra mounts and spare oxen with four other riders. A transport and a chuck wagon brought up the rear. Scouts rode ahead of the train, and the other riders flanked the wagons.

Leaving Independence was uneventful. The trail was well marked, with sets of dual tracks disappearing over the horizon. A sea of grass bounded the deeply etched trail as they set out. Spirits were high as the wagons lined up four abreast, traversing the well-trodden route.

At the first campsite on the trail, O'Brien called Jack aside. "From now on, don't ride your horse. Take one of the backups."

Jack asked, "Why?"

O'Brien smiled. "You'll see."

The next day, Jack noticed that all the men were riding backup horses. He unsaddled and turned Cutie loose to run with the remuda.

The terrain changed. Sparse oak trees, juniper, and mesquite gave way to blue grama, buffalo grass, and oak trees. Shimmering sunlight blurred the horizon.

As the wagon train approached the flatlands of Texas, O'Brien warned the scouts they were nearing Indian country and that the Indians were riled up because of the buffalo hunters slaughtering the herds. O'Brien's face flushed and his red hair seemed to brighten as he continued, "Kit Carson, with three hundred men, invaded the Comanche's country. The Indians routed them, but they're probably still angry."

Thirteen

Santa Fe Trail – Summer 1864

It was their third week on the trail. At breakfast, a night rider galloped into camp.

He yelled, "Five horses are missing!"

O'Brien calmly said, "Get some breakfast." He pointed at four of the men, and Jack. "Boys, get your best horses and follow me."

The men on horseback gathered around O'Brien. "Let's go!" O'Brien said, and with the men following, circled the remuda. All eyes scanned the ground.

Jack motioned to O'Brien and pointed at the barely noticeable tracks. "This way, boys."

The group urged their horses into a high trot. They followed the trail of the thieves through the grass-covered rolling plains. At midday, they crested a rise and spotted five Indians, each leading a stolen horse. O'Brien said, "Okay boys, let's get our horses back. Stay in line and follow me." He urged his horse into a run.

The Indians saw the approaching group and tried to urge their tired horses into a run. After a half mile, they turned the stolen horses loose. The men kept up the chase, forming a single line behind O'Brien. They continued to gain on the fleeing group because the Indians' spent horses were no match for the rested horses. The Indians had bows strung across their backs. Several grasped their weapon, tried to notch an arrow and turn to the right to fire at the pursuers— a difficult maneuver.

The chasers overtook the horse thieves on their right sides. Each pursuer pulled his revolver from its holster. One of the fleeing men twisted around in desperation and tried to shoot an arrow, but in his hurried movement he fell off his horse. A bullet through the head rewarded the grounded Indian. One at a time, the thieves fell from their horses, mortally wounded.

With the killing done, the group returned to a dead Indian. One of the crew yelled, "This one's mine." He jumped off his horse, grabbed the dead man's hair and with his knife cut a line across the corpse's forehead. He inserted his fingers into the cut and with a yank, separating the scalp from the head. A strip of skin at the neck of the victim was all that was attached to the dead Indian's head and with a skillful cut and a flick of the wrist, the man completed the task.

With the fresh scalp in his hand, he announced, "This will buy me five beaver pelts. All the tribes hate these Blackfeet and will want one on their coup sticks."

Jack gasped, "What the hell! You're no better than savages."

The scalper laughed. "Yeah, but I still got my hair."

The afternoon was spent gathering the gear and the scalps of the dead Indians. With the horses rounded up, the crew headed back to camp.

O'Brien rode next to Jack. "That's why we rest our best horses."

"I understand. But, scalping Indians?"

O'Brien massaged the back of his neck. "Laddie, I didn't make up the rules out here. The Blackfeet are outcasts in the Indian world. The reason we can travel across the trail unmolested is that we trade with all the other tribes, and they've heard stories about how us trappers settle up with thieves."

That night the cook announced, "You boys deserve a reward. Today I shot a deer, and I'm making deer camp fries." He explained how it's prepared. "Sliced tenderloin pieces, a quarter-inch thick, salt, pepper, and flour coating each piece, then deep fat fried 'til brown."

One wrangler asked, "You gonna feed us or talk us to death?"

One morning, O'Brien informed Jack that their next stop was north of a place called Adobe Walls. While the stock grazed and rested, Jack and one teamster would take the supply wagon and pick up fresh supplies of flour, coffee, and sugar. O'Brien estimated it would take three days for Jack to make the trip.

That night at camp, Jack said to O'Brien, "I haven't seen any Indians."

O'Brien chuckled, "They've been watching us for two days."

Curly added, "The Injuns have seen what happens when they attack us." The rest of the crew nodded. "If we had let the Blackfeet get away, word would spread that our livestock was easy pickings."

O'Brien said, "We're passing through Comanche and Kiowa country. We've been trading with them for many years. As long as we pass through peacefully, they'll not bother us."

The next morning, Jack and one of the teamsters driving the supply wagon headed for Adobe Walls. The teamster had made this trip before. "Jack, ride ahead to the next rise and make sure the way is clear."

The trip across the rolling sea of grass, under a bright sun, passed without incident. As they approached Adobe Walls, they saw that other travelers were also visiting. At the center of the compound was the trading post. They rode in and greeted the waiting proprietor. "Howdy, we were sent here by Sean O'Brien."

"Nice to see you. I've got the supplies O'Brien ordered on his way east. Any sign of Indians?"

"We haven't seen any, but O'Brien told us they've been watching us."

"O'Brien knows what he's talking about and has good relations with them. Some of those fellas outside are buffalo hunters, and they've stirred them up. Let's get you loaded and on your way."

The owner of the trading post scurried about, gathering their goods and loading the wagon. Jack and the teamster helped.

Jack wondered, *What's the hurry?*

The distant sound of gunfire answered his question.

Fourteen

Texas – Summer 1864

The collection of buildings that announced itself as Fort Worth was unimpressive. The mud-covered main street was bracketed by saloons, houses of ill repute and several stores with crudely painted signs advertising hunting supplies. Several places posted signs announcing the need for buffalo hunters and skinners. Ty had no desire to spend time in this town. He walked into a supply house that displayed the stars and bars of the Confederacy. At the counter, he addressed a pudgy shop keeper. "Your sign says you're looking for hunters."

"That's right, young fella. What experience do you have?"

"I spent the last year working on the King Ranch. Before that, I served as a sergeant in the 22nd Louisiana."

"I've heard of your outfit. I'd be pleased to have you as a member of one of my crews. The crew works as a team and splits the profit from the hunt equally."

Ty thought for a second. "That sounds good to me."

The shop keeper motioned to several rough-looking men. "That big fella with the feather in his hat is the leader of the crew." He yelled, "Joe Don, get over here."

Joe Don sauntered to the counter. "What do you want?"

"I've got you another hunter." He motioned toward Ty.

"What's your name?"

"Ty Jones."

"We'll be headed out the day after tomorrow. We're camped west of town. I'll be headed that way. You can follow me. Don't worry about food—it's supplied by the outfitter." He surveyed the pistols and rifle in Ty's hand. "You got ammunition for those guns?"

"Yes, sir."

"Okay, follow me."

As they exited the store, Ty thought, *What have I got myself into?*

Ty and his crew had been hunting buffalo near the Red River. The hunters rode ahead of the skinning crew. In one week, they had killed nearly one hundred buffalo. The joy the hunters showed with each buffalo's death disgusted Ty. He'd slaughtered animals for meat, but skinning the buffalo and leaving the meat to rot was wrong. Their wagons were full of skins, and the plains were littered with carcasses.

Comanche hunters from Quanah Parker's band had left their camp near the Washita River and headed across the plains looking for buffaloes. Meat for the winter needed to be secured. As the hunting party reached the Red River, they came across buffalo carcasses rotting on the plains. The putrid odor assaulted their nostrils.

It didn't take the Indians long to catch up with the skinning crew doing their grisly work. The Comanche could not understand why anyone would kill a buffalo, skin the animal, and leave the meat. This senseless slaughter incensed the Indians. They planned an attack.

The Comanche hunters divided their forces. One group would feign an attack on the skinners, while the second group made a loop around their prey and waited. The circling group stopped. One of their party shot an arrow straight up, signaling they were in position. The trailing band let loose a fuselage of arrows at the skinners. The butchers dropped their skinning knives and bolted for their wagons and jumped in. They beat their horses and pointed them to a nearby ravine where they thought they'd be able to hold off the attackers and wait for their riflemen to rescue them. The second group of Indians had set up a blockade just past the first turn in the ravine. The wagons met another hail of arrows. Several horses were struck, and the animals bucked and bolted. The skinners who survived the initial attack fell from the careening wagons.

Within minutes, the two groups of Indians converged on the stunned survivors and made short work of them with tomahawks and knives.

The hunting party, approximately one mile ahead of the skinning crew, heard the commotion and had spurred their horses to investigate. By the time the hunters spotted the wagons, the battle was over. All the hunters could do was turn tail and run for their lives.

An experienced hunter yelled, "Head for Adobe Walls." With the Indians a mile behind, the hunters spurred and beat their horses. As they approached Adobe Walls, they saw that other hunters had also taken refuge.

The Indians pulled up to survey the defenses. A runner was dispatched to tell Quanah Parker the situation and wait for instructions. After the hunting party's breathless description of the fate of the skinners, attention shifted to the Indians sitting on a hilltop overlooking their position. The assembled hunters and visitors prepared for an attack.

Fifteen

Adobe Walls – Summer 1864

Ty dismounted his horse and shook his head. He regretted joining the buffalo hunters, but he had never run away from a fight. He noticed that one man was standing by a wagon. Ty nodded at him and said to Jack, "Looks like we've brought trouble."

"From the looks of your Confederate holster, you've seen trouble before."

Ty looked at his horse. "That horse blanket looks like a Yankee issue."

Jack smiled and said, "It is, but the war is over for me." He extended his hand, "Jack Donaldson."

"Pleased to meet you. Ty Jones." Ty frowned and said, "I guess the war is over for both of us."

"Reckon so."

Ty shook his head. "I was at Vicksburg, and after we surrendered, I signed a letter saying I wouldn't fight the Union Army anymore, and I got paroled."

Jack scratched his head. "You fought for the Confederacy?"

Ty retorted, "That's right."

"I meant no offense. I didn't realize black men served in the Confederate Army."

"I was born a free man in Louisiana. When the war started, all the men my age joined to fight the northern invaders. During the Battle of Vicksburg, the other Rebel soldiers taunted us and said it was our fault the war started. Most of those fellas were uneducated crackers."

Jack nodded and explained, "I was at Gettysburg. Two of my lifelong friends were killed, one black and the other white. The Rebs' bullets were colorblind. After that slaughter, my enlistment was up, and I packed up. I could see no sense in continuing. Hell, half the Rebels didn't even have shoes. I figured the war was over."

Ty looked away. "The Confederacy will continue to fight while the generals still have people who are willing to die."

Jack added, "Being brought up on a farm in upstate New York, I guess I believed the gossip that the war would be over in two months. That was three years ago. I've had my bellyful of war. I guess we both have. And it looks like we left one war only to end up in another."

Ty and Jack pulled their rifles from their scabbards.

"We probably should take a position near the wall. Like it or not, I guess this is now our war."

The two men headed for the wall and surveyed the landscape. In the distance, they could see three Indians sitting on their horses looking at the fort.

Ty motioned his head toward the Indians. "Maybe we can end this war before it starts."

With that, Ty stated, "You've got a high-caliber Henry rifle. Why don't you aim at one of those Indians and take a shot?"

Jack smiled. "It's worth a try."

Ty shook his head. "If you can hit one of those Indians, I'll buy you a cigar."

Jack spent about half a minute lining up his shot. He breathed out as he applied pressure to the trigger, and the gunshot echoed across the plain. Nothing happened for nearly a half a minute. "Guess I missed."

As they looked up at the Indians, one fell off his horse.

When they saw the Indian fall, the other hunters let out a cheer. They could see the other Indians draping their fallen comrade over the back of his horse and leading it away. The rest of the war party followed as they headed south.

Ty motioned toward the hill. "Look at those Indians skedaddle. That was one hell of a shot."

Jack looked down. "I'm not proud that I've killed another man. Well, I guess you're going to get back to hunting buffalo."

Ty noticed Jack's hands shaking and said, "I'm tired of killing. That's why I'm heading west."

Jack stuffed his hands in his pockets. "Why don't you ride with me back to the wagon train? We're heading west. Maybe you can ride along."

Sixteen

Santa Fe Trail – Summer 1864

The trip to the wagon train was uneventful. Jack led the way with Ty by his side. The wagon with the supplies followed. Near dusk, they stopped, made camp, and ate.

Later that night, Jack and Ty talked about the war. Jack commented, "If Jeb Stuart was at Gettysburg on the first day with his cavalry, we could not have held the ridge. Our outfit was mounted infantry and didn't have much firepower."

Ty agreed. "We heard that General Lee was powerfully angry. Jeb was gallivanting around, raiding small towns, stealing chickens, and terrifying civilians."

Jack continued, "Lee was right to be mad at Stuart. By the third day of fighting, it was clear that the Rebs couldn't shake us loose. When our infantry got to the ridge with their long-range firing rifles, they fortified the position and lined up cannons. The tree line below Cemetery Ridge was about a mile away. The only way to attack was across an open field. You'd think Lee would call off the attack and live to fight another day. Those Reb soldiers lined up, shoulder to shoulder, and came a-marchin'. We slaughtered those brave men, and I picked up a bullet hole in the shoulder. After that my enlistment was up. I spent a short time in the hospital, then I headed home and visited with my family. I want to make a new life for myself in the west."

A sadness filled Ty's voice as he spoke. "General Grant just outfoxed us at Vicksburg. Once the Yank ships closed the Mississippi River and surrounded us, the battle was over. It took General Pemberton around forty days to figure it out. All Grant had to do was wait. More people died of starvation and typhoid than were killed by bullets. Food was scarce. By the end of the second week, we were eating rats and shoe leather. The Yanks outnumbered us two to one."

Jack grimaced. "When I joined up, a black man in my town wanted to serve. A sergeant told him the U.S. Army didn't want blacks, but the Confederate army accepted you. It makes no sense."

Ty nodded, saying, "You're right. After Vicksburg, I went home and talked to my father about the war. My dad thought slavery would die out on its own, as it has around the world. He knows a lot more about what's going on than I do. When I was growing up, he sheltered me from the reality of slavery. I swear I didn't realize how bad it was. I wanted to forget the war and go back to farming. But my dad believes that the South losing the war will only make it worse for black folks."

"I don't understand."

"Probably should have told you. My father is white. I don't fit in anywhere."

Jack stared at the fire. "If we own our own place, maybe we'll find a new life, and you'll fit in."

Ty answered, "It's worth a try." Both men spread out their bedrolls.

Seventeen

Santa Fe Trail – Summer 1864

The ride across the open plains was pleasant. A light breeze cooled them. Ty and Jack rode into camp with the wagon close behind. O'Brien met them in front of the circled wagons. As they approached, Jack said, "I'd like you to meet Ty Jones. He's heading west, and maybe he can ride along with us?"

O'Brien surveyed Ty. "Why would you want to do that?"

Ty dismounted. "I've had all the buffalo hunting I can stand."

O'Brien smiled and said, "I mean no offense, but you speak like a white man."

"White folks raised me. They treated me like I was one of them."

"Most folks think that all the blacks in the South are slaves."

"That's mostly true, but some of us, in Louisiana, were freeborn."

O'Brien extended his hand. "We could use another scout. You'll receive the same pay as all the others—one hundred dollars when we reach Santa Fe."

Ty gripped the outstretched hand. "Sounds like a good deal to me, Mr. O'Brien."

"The name's Sean. You'll be riding point with Jack. He'll show you the ropes. While we're in camp, you'll take your turn riding night herd and help repair wagons."

Two days later, O'Brien gathered all the men. "Okay lads, time to bring in the livestock and get hitched up. Jack, you take Ty and ride ahead to the next campsite. It's about ten miles due west. You'll recognize the spot by a stand of cottonwood trees near a small stream."

As Ty and Jack mounted their horses, they were facing east. The men sat transfixed. The gray dawn was being pushed out of the way by a rising sun, and the clouds transformed from a dull white to brilliant orange. Ty commented, "Ain't that a beautiful sight?"

O'Brien bellowed, "What are you two waiting for?"

The men turned their mounts and headed out of camp.

Ty glanced over his shoulder. "The sun's rising on a new day."

As they rode, Jack explained to Ty, "We have to follow the trail. The other guides are riding north and south of us.

They'll watch us. If there's any trouble, the other fellas will come a-runnin'. Kind of like that madman Custer."

Ty smiled, "I've heard of him. Didn't he say, 'charge' to the sound of the gunfire?"

"Yep. Someday Custer's gonna get a bunch of fellas killed." Both men nodded.

Eighteen

Santa Fe Trail – Summer 1864

They rode in silence for two hours. Each man occasionally glanced at the flanking companions. As they crested a small hill, Ty pointed. "That looks like the spot."

The campsite was two hundred feet off the trail. They waved at the other guides and turned toward the campsite.

Ty pulled up his horse. "Jack, we'd better go a little slow. I think there's an Indian sprawled out under that big cottonwood."

"By God, you've got good eyes."

The two men unlatched the safety on their pistol holsters and walked their horses to the fallen Indian.

Jack said, "You stay mounted with your pistol covering the Indian, and I'll get down and check him out."

Jack eased off his horse and drew his six-gun. He approached the Indian. Just then the other two guides arrived. Jack motioned them to stay back. He kneeled next to the Indian and placed his fingers on the fallen man's neck. He looked up at Ty. "He's got a pulse, might be knocked out. No, wait a minute, this fella's wounded."

One guide commented, "Why don't we finish him?"

Ty responded, "He's done us no harm."

Jack addressed the other guides, "You men ride back to the wagons and tell O'Brien what we've found. We'll stay here."

Without comment, the two guides wheeled their horses around, returned to the trail, and set off at a trot.

Ty dismounted and double-checked the Indian's pulse. "He's weak and has lost a fair amount of blood."

Jack nodded. "Let's bandage the wound and try to wake him up." After the men bandaged the wound, they propped the man against a tree and wiped his face with a wet dew rag. Slowly he revived. He opened his eyes, focused on Ty, and tried to reach for his knife. They had removed it from its scabbard.

Jack showed the Indian his knife and held his hands out. "I think he's a Comanche. Do you speak Indian?" Ty shook his head.

The Indian's lips curled at the edges. "Well, I speak the white man tongue."

Ty held out his canteen. "You better drink some water." The Indian frowned. Ty continued, "If we wanted to kill you, you'd already been dead."

The Indian nodded and accepted the canteen. After he drank his fill, he said to Ty, "My people call me Quanah." His alert eyes scanned the guides. Long black hair streamed down below his shoulders. His round face and high cheekbones hid his dual ancestry.

"My name's Ty, and my partner's name is Jack. You speak English well."

"My mother was a white woman."

Jack went to his horses and returned with several pieces of jerky and a biscuit. "You'd better eat something while we wait for the wagon train."

Ty and Jack unsaddled their horses. They retrieved brushes from their saddlebags and groomed their mounts. Quanah, his stomach full, closed his eyes and fell asleep.

Nineteen

Santa Fe Trail – Summer 1864

The wagon train came into sight, and they could see O'Brien spur his horse into a trot. The wagon master stopped in front of Ty and Jack, and dismounted. "Let's have a look at that Indian."

As the trio approached, Quanah opened his eyes. "Howdy, O'Brien. Your boys have been taking good care of me."

O'Brien smiled and looked at Quanah, "Glad you're still alive."

Jack spoke up. "You know this Indian?"

O'Brien turned and folded his arms across his chest. "This ain't any Indian. This here is Quanah Parker, Chief of the Comanches." Gazing at Quanah, he said, "How did you get yourself shot?"

"A couple of young warriors and I were looking for buffalo. We got jumped by some of Carson's soldiers, and they shot my young men in the back. I killed two of them, and the rest lit out." Quanah frowned. "They can't shoot good face to face. I was heading home. I got to this stream and got off my horse to get a drink. I guess I passed out."

O'Brien nodded, "You rest while I get the wagon train settled and tend to the livestock. I'll be back. We have a doctor traveling with us. I'll send him to look at that wound."

The wagons formed up in the same arrangement each night. The men tended to the oxen, greased the wheel bearings, and set up tents and sleeping pallets. Some men gathered wood while the cook prepared the evening meal.

As the men lined up by the chuck wagon, O'Brien remarked, "Ty and Jack, after you get your plate, come over to where Quanah is. I'll bring him a plate."

Jack and Ty followed O'Brien. Quanah tried to stand.

O'Brien barked, "Stay seated. I've brought you food."

After the men sat, balancing plates on their lap, they ate. Jack asked O'Brien, "You and Quanah seem to be acquainted?"

"We've known each other for many years. Quanah saved my scalp. I was out trapping and didn't realize I was in Crow country. Quanah and some of his warriors surrounded the Crow camp just as they were getting ready to lift my hair. Quanah's men killed three of the Crows, the others hightailed it, and I got to keep my hair."

Quanah smiled. "The Crows were in Comanche country."

O'Brien continued, "After that, I spent a couple of weeks in Quanah's camp. We talked about how the country was changing." He paused and looked at Quanah. "The Comanches know the white men are coming, and permit me to travel through their country, so long as I don't slaughter the buffaloes."

Jack smiled. "Your hair would make a nice decoration to an Indian spear."

O'Brien chuckled, "Well, they'll just have to wait a while." The men resumed eating.

Quanah was the first to speak. "My people have known for a long time about the whites. We don't hate the white man. My mother is white. The old men told me about the first whites; they were Spanish. The Spaniards with iron hats got lost. They roamed around the plains, gave up, and went back to Mexico. The elders tell me that's how our people got horses. The iron hats abandoned their horses, and we captured them. We're grateful for that. Many whites die because they don't respect the land."

Ty and Jack sat listening while the two old friends were talking. Ty asked, "Why did your people attack the buffalo hunters?"

Quanah clasped his hands together and made a chopping motion as he talked. "Those hunters have no respect for the buffalo or the land. Every time they come onto our land, they leave a trail of rotting carcasses and filth. They shoot mama cows and leave the calves to starve or to be killed by wolves. More whites will be coming. If they pass through peacefully, we'll leave them alone."

The next day the wagons were made ready for that day's march. Ty and Jack rode over to say goodbye to Quanah. The chief was up and looked rested. As they approached, Quanah raised his hand in a sign of peace. "You men saved my life."

Ty answered, "We're glad to help. We've seen enough killing to last a lifetime. We just wanted to see if you're up for your trip home."

Quanah smiled. "I'll be fine." He added, "You men are always welcome in my village."

Ty and Jack turned their horses and rode out of camp. Jack commented, "I wonder what's ahead of us?"

"Let's go find out." The partners urged their horses into a fast trot.

Twenty

Santa Fe Trail – Fall 1864

There were several rivers to cross. It was a treacherous undertaking. At the Canadian River, O'Brien called everyone together. He began, "Boys, tomorrow we cross the Canadian River. I've made this crossing several times. Each crossing was different. In the spring, the rush of water changes the river's depth and the banks. Tomorrow, I'll cross on horseback and scope out the river. When I determine the proper place to cross, I'll plant stakes. Your job is to make sure the wagons stay between the stakes. Once we begin to cross, I'll tell you when it's your turn. I want no shenanigans during the crossing. Everyone attached to a wagon will wade to the left of their wagon—guides will ride with you in case there's any problem. Everyone should get a good night's sleep. Tomorrow is going to be a long day."

The next morning everyone was up before dawn. While they ate, O'Brien assigned guides to lead each team of oxen. Ropes were to be tied around the lead ox's horns, and the driver would walk alongside with his whip and direct the crossing with voice commands. Flankers were detailed to ride beside the prairie schooners and were told to tie their lassos through stanchions between the front and rear wheels of the wagon.

O'Brien finished the assignments with a note of caution: "The beds of the wagons are waterproofed with oil and paint and will float if necessary, but let's hope it doesn't happen. If a wagon looks like it ain't gonna make it, unhitch the oxen and cut the lassos. I've never lost a load. If we need to, we'll salvage the rig downstream."

Followed by the guides, O'Brien rode to the river. He bellowed, "I'm first. Wait here."

With that, he nudged his horse's flank and eased him into the water. To his surprise, the river was lower than he expected. After crossing the river, O'Brien placed the stakes. All the guides not assigned to a wagon were posted in the river to help if needed. First, the livestock crossed the river, then the chuck wagon, and finally the freight wagons.

O'Brien sat on his horse on the other side of the river, watching each crossing. When needed he'd yell, "Take the slack out of that rope! Mind those oxen! Stay between the stakes! You ain't going to town; take your time!"

When all the livestock and wagons had crossed, O'Brien directed the men to make camp and check for damage. "We'll get underway at first light. Good job today."

As the wagon train crossed into New Mexico, the mountains in the distance grew larger with each passing day. At camp, O'Brien called all the guides together. He pointed west and said, "Now starts the trickiest part. We've got to navigate through Raton Pass. I've traveled the pass probably twenty times and like the rivers, each time it's different. We're here before winter sets in and that's a good thing—look at those peaks. That's snow. In two days, we're going to stop to rest the stock, grease and soak every wagon wheel, check the undercarriages, and mend harnesses."

The first day on the Raton Pass trail was a challenge. Several wagons needed assistance on the ascent. Guides tied their ropes on the axles and dallied their lassos around the horns of their saddles. The oxen strained, and the horses dug their hind legs into the task.

O'Brien watched every tow. He spotted guides dismounting and walking behind a wagon, trying to push. He yelled, "Get the hell away from the back of that wagon and stay on your horse. If that wagon breaks loose, you'll all be dead."

Twenty-One

—◆◆◆◆◆◆—

Santa Fe, New Mexico – Fall 1864

When the wagon train was five miles from Santa Fe, O'Brien called everyone together. "We're at the end of the trail. We'll get into Santa Fe by noon tomorrow. We'll settle up tonight."

O'Brien sat down by Ty and Jack's campfire. "Well men, this is it. You've earned your pay." With that, he counted out one hundred dollars for each man, half in gold coins and half in U.S. dollars. "After I hold up for a couple of days, I figure I'll head north and do some trapping. Would you men like to tag along?"

Jack and Ty exchanged glances. Ty answered, "We've been thinking about starting a ranch. We're not sure where but the war will be over soon, and folks will be wanting beef."

O'Brien smiled and said, "You're probably right. I wish you well. You might want to look up a feller by the name of Charley Goodnight. I think he's got the same plan." He stood, extended his hand to Ty, and commented, "You're a hell of a guide." Smiling at Jack, he remarked, "For a feller that didn't know anything, you did a great job."

Jack smiled and said, "You keep your hair attached."

O'Brien nodded. "I'll try."

After O'Brien departed, Jack remarked, "Maybe tomorrow we can look up Goodnight and see what he's up to."

The two men rolled out their bedrolls and slept through the night.

The next day they accompanied the wagons to the town square in Santa Fe and bid their good-byes to their traveling companions, especially to Woody for the great meals he prepared along the trail.

Jack said, "We've been sleeping out. It would be nice to spend a few nights with a roof over our head."

Ty shook his head. "They probably won't let me stay with white folks."

"It doesn't hurt to ask. Let's wet our whistles first."

They stopped in the local cantina and approached the bar. Ty smiled and asked the bartender for two beers.

The bartender looked up. "I won't serve no black. I fought for the Confederacy."

Jack's pronouncement shocked the bartender: "So did he," pointing to Ty.

The man behind the bar asked, "What unit?"

"Army of Mississippi, 22nd Louisiana Detachment."

With the beers served, the bartender asked, "You at Vicksburg?"

"Yes, sir. How much for the beers?"

The bartender responded, "Nothing."

Ty asked the bartender, "We're looking for a man named Goodnight."

A tall man wearing a tall hat approached. "My name's Goodnight. I overheard your conversation. Pleased to meet you." His pants were stuffed in the top of a long pair of cowboy boots. He wore a black jacket and a white shirt with a black string tie. A large cigar was gripped between his teeth.

Ty and Jack looked at each other. Jack asked, "Are you Charley Goodnight?"

He removed his cigar, "Who told you my name was Charley?"

"Sean O'Brien from the wagon train. We just got into town today."

"He knows I hate to be called Charley, so call me Charles. How's that old rascal?" Smiling, he returned his cigar to its place of prominence.

Ty responded, "He's one hell of a wagon master. I think he's headed north to do some trappin' over the winter."

Goodnight smiled. "I hope he keeps his hair." The men laughed. "What brings you west?"

"We told Mr. O'Brien we were thinking about starting a cattle ranch. He suggested we hook up with you."

"Do you have any experience with cattle?"

Ty answered, "I worked on the King Ranch down in the Rio Grande Valley for a year."

Jack added, "We've been talking about this during the trip here. Ty even showed me how to handle a rope."

Goodnight's face lit up. "Well, that's a start."

Goodnight spent the next hour describing his plan to go to the Texas/Mexican border and buy cows. He was assembling a group of at least eighteen cowboys, supplies, and remounts. The wage for the round trip was two hundred dollars per man.

Ty asked, "Mr. Goodnight, could Jack and I spend a minute discussing your offer?"

"Sure."

Jack and Ty walked outside to discuss the offer. When they returned, Jack spoke, "We plan to start our own ranch. Would you mind if we took half the pay in money and the balance in cattle?"

Goodnight rubbed his fleshy chin, "Okay, we'll settle up at one dollar per head. That gets you two hundred cows. I'll throw in five bulls."

Ty and Jack nodded, saying, "Deal." The men shook hands and ordered more beers. When the bartender deposited the beers on their table, Goodnight asked, "How much?" The bartender turned his back and walked back to the bar. "You'll drink on the house as long as that man from the 22nd is with you."

Goodnight added, "I also fought for the Confederacy."

The bartender responded, "I know that. But the men at Vicksburg went through hell. The black soldiers did themselves proud."

Goodnight explained that they would head out at the end of next week. He asked, "You fellas have a place to stay?"

Jack responded, "No."

"The Rancho Nambe has rooms. Some of my men are staying there. Let's go see if there's room for two more."

Twenty-Two

Santa Fe, New Mexico – Fall 1864

As they entered the hotel's registration lobby, Goodnight smiled and asked, "Cómo estás, Oscar?"

"Muy bien, Charles." Oscar Morales extended his hand. He stood five feet, five inches. His grip strengthened by years of hard work, he gently clasped his old friend's hand.

"It looks like you've gained some weight."

Oscar responded, "The sign of a good wife."

The men chuckled. Oscar's wife joined him and jabbed him in his ribs. Her combed-back, graying hair was tied with a ribbon. Her perfect smile filled out her attractive, olive-skinned face. A work apron covered a cotton dress. The men removed their hats and nodded.

Goodnight continued in English, "These two men are coming with me when I head south to buy cattle. Can you find room for them?"

"Sí, Charles." Oscar looked at Ty and Jack. "My daughter will show you to your room." In a booming voice, he yelled, "Esmeralda!"

A dark-haired girl standing five feet tall glided into the room. "Sí, Papa." Her raven eyes settled on Jack. After a slight smile, she averted her glance.

"Show these men to the room near the stable."

Esmeralda's radiant smile captivated the men. Her beauty was a gift from her mother. She motioned for them to follow her. At the room, she opened the door and stood with downcast eyes as she motioned for them to enter. Jack turned around to watch Esmeralda scurry back to her Papa.

Jack commented, "She's beautiful. Hope to see her again."

Ty grinned. "I wonder if she'd like to spend some time with me?"

Each day the crew assembled for breakfast, and the women cooked and served.

Jack caught Esmeralda's eye the first morning and nodded. She brought his breakfast and smiled. "Is your room comfortable?"

Jack turned bright red and said, "It's perfect."

Ty waited for her to leave and asked, "Did I get all the spiders and crickets in my bed?"

Jack poked him in the ribs.

Jack and Esmeralda's morning meetings at breakfast expanded into pleasant conversation. One morning, Jack asked, "Would you walk with me this evening?"

She smiled and said, "We can walk to the square after dinner."

As she walked away, Ty asked, "Can I come along?"

Jack answered, "No."

Twenty-Three

Santa Fe, New Mexico – Fall 1864

Each morning, Goodnight assembled his crew. Duties for the day were assigned. One morning Goodnight said, "Ty and Jack, come with me."

As they walked out of the room, four cowboys joined them. The partners saddled their horses. Goodnight looked at the assembled crew. "Make sure your rifles and pistols are loaded." Goodnight waited until each man checked his weapons.

Jack turned and blew a kiss to Esmeralda; she blushed and smiled. Ty grasped his heart, slumped in his saddle, and laughed.

As they headed out of town, Goodnight explained, "I've made a deal with some comancheros to buy extra horses for the trip, and we'll meet them at Apache Canyon." They urged their horses into a trot. They covered the five miles in just over one hour.

At the head of the canyon, a group of men sat waiting. The crew stopped, and Goodnight turned to face the group. "Unstrap your pistols and stay ready."

The horse sellers were a rough-looking bunch, with dirty clothes and unkempt beards ranging from scraggly to full. Two of the crew had no beards and wore a combination of Indian and cowboy garb. Goodnight addressed the leader, a rotund man with a smile that highlighted his scraggly teeth. "How are you, Frenchie?"

"Waiting on you." Frenchie's dirty, broken teeth were almost covered by an overgrown mustache and a shaggy beard. His head was covered by a skunk-skin cap that sat atop his crimson and black hair. A leather belt with a gold buckle surrounded his deerskin blouse and pants. He sat on a paint horse with a silver-trimmed Mexican saddle.

"You got the horses?"

"Yup, up at the canyon."

Goodnight responded, "Times a-wastin'." With that, the comancheros turned and headed up the pinyon pine and cactus-filled valley. A half-mile into the canyon, a corral made out of old cedar posts and strands of twisted barbed wire held nearly four hundred horses.

Goodnight explained, "Frenchie, your boys will push the horses out of the corral one at a time. Ty, you and Jack will go to the head of the canyon and hold all the horses that are headin' your way."

He turned to the other four cowboys. "I'm going to yell pass or back. Only the horses I pass are allowed down the canyon."

The sorting process took the better part of three hours. During the sort, Frenchie and Goodnight argued about the horses. When the sorting was complete, Goodnight settled up.

Goodnight looked at Frenchie and said, "You and your boys stay right here until we're clear."

A broad smiled filled Frenchie's face. "You worried?"

"If you try to steal back these horses, I'll tie you on the back of a mule and take you back to Canada where the Mounties will hang you."

Frenchie's smile disappeared as Goodnight and his men rode to join Ty and Jack.

The trip back to Santa Fe was uneventful. The crew corralled the horses outside of town, and men were assigned to guard the new mounts. Ty, Jack, and two others drew the first two-hour shifts.

Jack asked Ty, "You've worked on a ranch. What do you think happens next?"

"Beats me."

The relief showed up on time.

"Any problems?"

"No." Ty added, "Why do you ask?"

"Goodnight told us to keep our eyes open. I don't think you fellas noticed, but about ten of the horses he turned back had Goodnight's brand. The boss told me he'd be damned if he'd buy horses stolen from him. Frenchie and the boss had one hell of an argument while you fellas were waiting. Frenchie is smart enough not to push Goodnight too far."

Twenty-Four

Santa Fe, New Mexico – Fall 1864

The next day, all the cowboys gathered around the corral. Each man had been instructed to bring two lariats.

Goodnight addressed the cowboys, "Each of you will get two new horses as extra mounts. These horses are pretty rough. You'll have three days to break them. We leave on Monday."

The head wrangler, a fellow named Clint, gathered two ropes and entered the enclosure. "Jack, you're first. Stand next to me."

Jack stood while Clint roped two horses. He handed the ropes to Jack. Clint hollered, "Ty, you're next."

Ty and Jack exchanged glances as they entered the corral. Jack remarked, "I ain't never seen a rope thrown like that."

"That backhand toss is called a Houlihan. The foreman at the King Ranch roped horses like that." They watched as each horse was roped. "He never misses."

That night, Goodnight sat with Ty and Jack. "I told Clint to pick out the calmest horses for you boys."

The next day, the partners took their horses to a corral and saddled the first horse. Ty smiled and said, "That's one of yours." Jack gingerly put his foot into the stirrup and swung onto the horse's back. Ty released the reins, and the horse just stood his ground.

Jack asked, "What's next?"

"Get him to move."

Jack gently spurred the horse, and off they went. After completing a circle and reversing to a stop, Jack jumped off. "You're next."

Jack held the bridle as Ty saddled his horse and mounted. As Jack released his hold, the horse lowered his head and bucked. The surprised look soon disappeared as Ty landed on the ground flat on his back.

Jack looked at Ty; they both laughed. Jack commented, "I guess we know who the real cowboy is."

"We'll see."

They worked on their horses throughout the day. Jack got bucked off his next horse. That night at dinner, Goodnight asked, "How'd you boys make out?"

Ty answered, "A little sore, but we'll live."

Goodnight speared a piece of steak. "I'm glad Clint picked out gentle horses for y'all."

Ty and Jack exchanged glances and went back to eating. Ty commented, "I broke horses at the King Ranch."

As he chewed, Goodnight spoke, "King's horses ain't nothing compared to these mustangs. A little advice. Get a forty-foot lead rope and attach it to the horse's halter. Get him running in a circle by slapping a whip on the ground behind the horse. Make him run at least forty revolutions, turn the horse in the other direction by slapping a whip on the ground and don't hit him. It'll take the horse a while to catch on. Once the horse is good and tired, let him stop. Walk up and stand by him. Pet his withers and neck." He swallowed his steak and speared another piece and continued, "The next day do the same thing with a saddle on his back. When he walks up to you, pet him. Bounce the stirrups against his side, not enough to hurt. Put your foot in the stirrup, jump up, then step down. Do this until the animal is calm, then swing your leg over and sit. All the while, your partner will be holding the lead rope. Walk the horse around for ten minutes."

Jack asked, "Will this break the horse to ride?"

"Maybe, but you can work the animal when we camp at night. You'll figure out when the horse is ready."

The men finished their meal in quiet.

Goodnight told them, "You boys get yourselves a good winter coat and warm gloves."

Jack asked, "Why do we need heavy clothes? I thought the desert was always hot."

Goodnight laughed. "You'll see."

《‧‧◆‧‧》

That night, Jack met Esmeralda, saying, "Would you mind if we sat and talked?"

"Okay. What's bothering you?"

"I think the horses are breaking me."

She smiled and clasped his hand. Jack spent the night talking about his plans for the ranch. He exclaimed, "What would make this perfect is if you were with me."

"You'll have to talk to Papa."

"Is that yes?"

She kissed his cheek.

"We're going south with Goodnight to buy cattle. As soon as I return, I'll talk to your papa."

She smoothed his hair and wrapped her arms around him, "Mi amor. We must get back to the hotel."

《‧‧◆‧‧》

The next two days passed quickly. Ty and Jack made progress with their horses, as preparations were made for riding south.

The day they would head out, Jack took Esmeralda's hand after breakfast and spirited her to an alcove.

"We're leaving tomorrow, but I'll be back." He pulled her close. "I love you."

Esmeralda kissed him. "I'll be waiting."

Twenty-Five

New Mexico Territory – Winter 1864

One cowboy commented as the group formed up, "I've got a good way to break that roan horse of mine. A bullet through the head."

Jack nodded at him. "Maybe you should talk to Mr. Goodnight."

Six cowboys were detailed to herd the extra horses. Goodnight rode to the front and headed south at a slow pace, following the well-marked trail. Six wranglers pushed the herd. The chuck wagon and a prairie schooner carrying supplies followed. The remaining cowboys settled into a loose formation flanking the herd and wagons.

The trail ran parallel to the Rio Grande River. The country changed as they headed south—snow-covered mountains and grassy valleys gave way to cactus, salt cedars, and a beige desert.

Ty and Jack rode together. "I thought the desert was hot."

Jack answered, "Me too." The men wrapped mountain man buffalo coats tight around themselves and buried their hands in fur-lined gloves.

On the first night, Clint assigned each man his shift to ride night herd. Ty and Jack constructed a high line between the chuck wagon and the supply wagon. The horses to be kept saddled throughout the night were fed, watered, and their halters tied to the new line. Woody prepared the evening meal.

Goodnight spoke to the assembled cowboys. "Being this close to Santa Fe, I don't expect we'll have any problem with Indians but keep an eye out for Frenchie and his crew. If you see them, shoot first."

On the third night, a gunshot brought the cowboys out of their bedrolls. The shots came from the direction of the horse herd. They sprang into already-saddled horses and arrived in time to see the horses stampeding away with the night herders close behind. They spotted five rustlers heading north.

Goodnight bellowed, "Half of you, follow Clint and help run down the horses. The rest of you follow me."

Ty looked at Jack and said, "To the sound of the gunfire."

Within minutes, Cutie carried Jack to the head of the group. He spotted the riders and gave chase. Ty and Goodnight caught up. Their horses were fresh. The rustlers' mounts were tired. They were gaining on the band of rustlers. Goodnight yelled, "Jack, you were a mounted rifleman, show me what you can do."

Jack tied a knot in the reins and let them fall on his horse's neck. He reached down and pulled out his carbine. Cutie maintained a flat-out run as Jack stood in his stirrups and shot at the last man of the fleeing rustlers. The man slumped in the saddle and fell. As he fell, he grasped the saddle horn and pulled his horse over.

Goodnight, Jack, and Ty pulled up next to the downed desperado. Goodnight jumped off his horse and placed his fingers on the fallen rider's neck. "Dead as a doornail." As he turned over the corpse, Goodnight shook his head and muttered, "Oh my God. I recognize this boy."

Ty and Jack approached the fallen horse. Ty remarked, "The horse has a broken leg." He aimed his carbine between the horse's eyes and pulled the trigger, ending the animal's pain.

Goodnight stated, "Frenchie's crew won't be back anytime soon. You boys, help me lift this body onto my horse. His father is a vaquero for Valdez. Damn that Frenchie for leading this young man astray!"

Without further comment, Ty and Jack secured the body to Goodnight's saddle. Goodnight mounted behind the seat and kept his hand on the dead boy's back.

The men returned to camp. The other cowboys were waiting. Goodnight asked, "How'd you boys do?"

Clint answered, "We didn't lose any. It looks like you've brought one back with you."

Goodnight motioned to Clint, "Look at the boy's face."

Clint lifted the dead man's head. "Oh mercy, this is the son of one of Valdez's vaqueros."

"Let's give him a decent burial."

Without comment, Goodnight and Clint untied the body and carried it to an open spot. Ty and Jack followed them with shovels.

After the burial, Jack and Ty were sitting quietly as Goodnight approached. Jack remarked, "I had no idea."

"You did nothing wrong. Frenchie's going to pay for this."

Clint asked, "Who shot the boy?"

Goodnight replied, "On horseback at a run, Jack shot the man dead center."

The cowboys hearing the exchange nodded. Goodnight continued, "We're out of here at first light. Don't think we'll be seeing Frenchie's men again, but stay alert."

Jack and Ty lingered behind. Jack's hands shook. Ty put his hand on his partner's shoulder. "You're a hell of a good man. If killing didn't bother you, I wouldn't be your partner."

"I guess you got to do what you got to do."

Twenty-Six

New Mexico Territory – Winter 1864

The next two days were uneventful. On the fifth night out, Goodnight sat with Ty and Jack and asked, "How are you boys doing?"

Ty answered, "Doing great. Our new horses have settled down."

Jack added, "I'm glad we bought these winter coats. It's cold enough for mittens."

Goodnight chuckled and replied, "Glad to hear it. Nothing hurts like getting bucked off in cold weather."

Jack commented, "I thought we'd run into Indians by now."

Goodnight nodded. "We would have, but Kit Carson and the Union Army are relocating them."

After breakfast, as the outfit was getting ready to move out, an army patrol entered the camp.

Goodnight snarled, "What do you fellas want?"

The young lieutenant saluted. "Sir. We're with General Carson's command."

"Don't you salute me, sonny. What's Carson up to?"

"Sorry. General Carson sent me to find you."

Goodnight held his hand up. "Don't apologize. It's a sign of weakness."

The flustered officer answered, "General Carson asked me to invite you to our camp for a visit."

"I ain't takin' time to visit Carson. You can tell him I'm headin' south. If Carson wants to see me, he can track me down. Good day to you."

As the patrol rode out of camp. The lieutenant commented, "The general can deal with that man." The old sergeant riding with him noted, "The general knows Goodnight, they ain't no friends."

The next day's campsite was by the banks of the Rio Grande River, in a thicket of trees and brush surrounded by barren land. A detachment of soldiers approached the camp. At its head rode Kit Carson. He sat his horse comfortably. His five-foot-six-inch frame sat under a sizeable, well-shaped head covered with reddish hair that complemented his freckled face.

Goodnight, with his cigar firmly in place, snarled, "I see you got promoted."

Carson's soft blue eyes scanned Goodnight. "Nice to see you again, Colonel."

"I ain't a colonel. What do you want?"

Carson frowned. "The army's relocated a couple of thousand Navajos to a new reservation by Bosque Redondo. I'd like you to buy some beefs down south and deliver them to the new reservation."

"You and General Carleton picked the wickedest place to locate a reservation. A self-respecting lizard wouldn't live there. Why don't you just shoot them?" Without hesitation, he continued, "How many beefs do you want?"

Carson glared at Goodnight. "About one thousand head." After a short pause, "Will you do it or not?"

"Ten dollars a cow, in gold, not Yankee paper money."

"Agreed. When can I expect the cattle?"

"Thirty to forty days. We'll drive the cows to Santa Fe. You can have one of your soldiers at Santa Fe tell you when we arrive."

With no further comment, Carson wheeled his horse and rode off, his detachment hurrying to catch up.

Ty commented to Jack, "They don't like each other."

That night at camp, the off-duty cowboys sat around the campfire drinking coffee. Clint asked, "Mr. Goodnight, Carson called you colonel. I didn't know you were in the army?"

Goodnight looked at Clint. "I served the Confederacy, same as Ty, but I weren't no colonel. I was a lieutenant with the 2nd Texas Mounted Rifle Battalion. I nearly killed Carson at the Battle of Val Verde. His horse saved him."

Goodnight went on, "At a river crossing, I had Carson in my sights but my horse spooked and I missed. The last time I saw Carson, he looked me dead in the eye and spurred his horse and rode like hell up an embankment. The only way the Yankees beat us was by sneaking in our camp and burning our supplies. The damn blue bellies are good at starving people to death."

He smiled and continued, "Carson is fired up about the Injuns because his Cheyenne wife divorced him."

Clint scratched his head, "Carson has one hell of a reputation."

Goodnight expelled a cloud of cigar smoke and stated, "He's earned his reputation. I don't like him, but I respect him. He's tough as an old boot."

Twenty-Seven

Las Cruces, New Mexico — Winter 1864

The barren land offered no relief. Each day presented a new challenge. The bone-chilling cold was followed by blinding sun. Relief came at sundown, as an ever-changing show of colors filled the western sky. Each man had his own sleeping bag. Pieces of canvas sewn with buffalo gut made an airtight compartment for thick blankets. The only things a man took off at night were his boots and hat. Many men had fashioned a skull cap to keep the chill off their heads. It was better to ride upwind from the cowboys.

By three in the morning, the crew was up and ready to move. The men traveled until just after sunup and had a breakfast of coffee, biscuits, and bacon. At noon, before the sun was at its zenith, the camp was established near the river. The livestock was fed grain and turned loose to scavenge for any green vegetation they could find. The cowboys rode herd in two-hour shifts. All rested under tarps mounted on tent poles. At sundown, the cook served the day's main meal.

Some cowboys grumbled about the beans, salt pork, and biscuits. Woody replied, "If you don't like it, I'll throw it to the hogs."

From the crew, someone commented, "Good, we'll eat the hogs."

The old cook grabbed his carving knife. "Who said that?"

The men laughed as they lined up with their plates.

The long trip ended. On a hill overlooking Las Cruces, the band made camp. At dinner, Goodnight told the men, "Tomorrow I'm gonna ride into town and hunt up Sancho Valdez and see if the old cattle rustler has any cows for sale. I'm gonna see if the Rio Grande Hotel has rooms available. Y'all stay put until I get back."

The foreman set up the guard rotation, with a warning: "Ole man Valdez ain't above having his men stealing our horses while he's negotiating with the boss."

Duties assigned, some men curry-brushed their horses, and others lounged by the chuck wagon.

Valdez sat outside his favorite cantina. His sombrero lay on the back of his silver hair; his weathered face told the story of a rugged life. His full-lipped, mustached mouth broke into a wide smile as Goodnight approached. "No ha muerto aún?"

Goodnight smiled, "No, ain't dead yet. You'll beat me to hell."

"That is good. When you get there, I'll rustle some cattle and have them waiting for you."

Goodnight dismounted and took a seat at Valdez's table.

"Quiero una cerveza?"

"I've been spittin' cotton for the last hundred miles."

Valdez motioned for the waiter to bring another beer. "How is the war with the Yankees going?"

"It's all over, except no one knows it." Goodnight continued, "I'm looking for around three thousand cows."

"I found some."

"I'm sure you have. Where did you find them?"

Valdez smiled. "Near Chihuahua, running free—no brands."

"Where are they?"

"In my valley."

"What's the price?"

"For my old friend, only two dollars per cow."

"How much do your enemies pay?"

What followed was a lengthy negotiation, enhanced by several beers. As the sun sank, they agreed on a dollar a cow.

Valdez finished the negotiation. "No paper, only gold."

"Done." Goodnight handed Valdez a cigar. A cloud of smoke and a shot of tequila sealed the deal. The men agreed to meet in two days at Valdez's headquarters five miles west of Las Cruces.

Before they separated, Goodnight asked, "Where does José live?"

"Why?"

Goodnight explained. Valdez said, "I'll take you."

Goodnight told José, with his hat in hand, what happened to his son.

José, crestfallen said, "Thank you, mi amigo. Mi two sobrions rode north with my boy." He called out, "Ven aqui." His wife joined him at the door. Goodnight and Valdez stepped back as José explained what had happened. Her eyes blazed in anger, and as José continued, a mask of grief replaced rage.

She looked at Goodnight. No words could describe her silent message. She walked into her house and returned with a scarf covering her head and rosary beads clutched to her breast. She gently grasped her husband's hand and guided him up the hill to their church.

Goodnight watched the grief-stricken couple, and they seemed to shrink under their burden. He threw his cigar to the ground and said to Valdez, "That Frenchie deserves to rot in hell."

Twenty-Eight

Las Cruces, New Mexico – January 1865

For the next two days, the crew lived in the Rio Grande Hotel. It was a two-story adobe building with a porch and balcony. The men had to double up but were grateful for a chance to sleep in a bed and use the communal bath. Tasty meals prepared for them by Mexican cooks filled the cowboys' stomachs.

On the third day, they set out. The river valley west of Las Cruces provided a welcome relief from the desert. Water for green crops and pecan orchards was supplied by irrigation ditches from the Rio Grande. After a five-mile ride, the crew entered a mile-long grass valley. Cows grazed or rested in the noonday sun.

Valdez's camp and corrals occupied a strip of land at the entrance of the valley. Off in the distance, vaqueros could be seen guarding the herd.

The crew rode to the camp. Valdez mounted his horse and met the men.

"Hola, Goodnight."

Goodnight answered, "It looks like you've got more than enough cattle."

"Sí, my friend, more cattle show up all the time."

The crew all chuckled. Goodnight said, "We'll have to run them through your work chutes. I need to sort off the old and lame. We have a long trip ahead of us."

"No hay problema. It'll take a couple of days. You can camp near the river."

Duties were agreed. Valdez's crew would sort the cows into groups of one hundred and drive them to the chutes. Goodnight's team would work them into the holding area. Goodnight would inspect each cow. Cows that met with his approval were sorted into pens, and the rejects were turned loose and kept away from the unprocessed cattle by Valdez's vaqueroes.

Both crews sat on their horses while Goodnight and Valdez argued.

Ty asked his foreman, "How long will this go on?"

"Those two old buzzards can argue like this for days."

Finally, Goodnight reached into his pocket and handed Valdez a cigar.

The foreman commented, "That does it. The deal's settled."

At night, Valdez's cook prepared a feast of refried beans, fajitas, and fresh tortillas. During the meal, Valdez motioned to Ty, "Cuanto quieres para tu caballo?"

Ty answered, "No para la venta."

Jack asked, "What was that all about?"

"He wants to buy my horse. I told him he wasn't for sale."

"Where did you learn Spanish?"

"From my father, and I had a little practice while you were chasing Esmeralda."

After dinner, bottles of mescal were passed around, and the crews enjoyed a boisterous good time.

The next day before dawn, Clint walked through camp. Groggy eyes slowly opened. "Okay boys, play cowboy all night, play cowboy all day."

Groans greeted the foreman.

Jack's weary eyes focused on Ty. "I ain't never drank mescal."

Ty responded, "My first and last time."

After a breakfast of coffee, tortillas, and refried beans, the crew mounted and took their places by the work chutes. Several men turned green and deposited their breakfast on the ground.

An afflicted cowboy uttered, "That Mexican whiskey goes down white and comes out green."

Twenty-Nine

New Mexico Territory – January 1865

Valdez's crew helped push the herd out of the valley. The cattle moved at a slow, deliberate pace. Goodnight and Valdez rode in front.

After they cleared the valley, the open prairie stretched toward the rising sun. As the herd passed, Goodnight and Valdez sat and watched—sharing the moment.

Valdez's vaqueros gathered around. Goodnight waved, "Vaya con Dios."

Valdez smiled and asked, "Same time next year?"

Goodnight frowned. "Only if you reduce your price," then he smiled. "See you next year." He spurred his horse into a trot and made his way to the front of the herd.

The first day of the drive ended five miles north of Las Cruces. The cattle settled in a grass-covered plain near the Rio Grande. The camp was set up and night herders assigned.

The cowboys got their plates and ate. Goodnight asked, "Anyone want some mescal?" The only sound heard was a coyote howling in the distance. The cowboys finished eating and spread out their bedrolls.

At breakfast, Goodnight gathered the crew. "Clint will assign your place around the herd. Each day, your positions will rotate. Two of you will ride the point with me. Two of you will ride drag. The rest of you will ride the flanks. The chuck and supply wagons will ride ahead, and the horse herd will follow the wagons."

The cowboys removed the horses' hobbles. The wagons headed north.

Goodnight, with his two riders, waited until the cattle bunched up behind them. Clint shouted, "Move 'em out!"

Ty and Jack were assigned drag. A cloud of dust engulfed them. They covered fifteen miles on the first day. Ty and Jack rode into camp covered with trail dust. Clint said, "Y'all wash off in the river, and we'll save you supper. Your night herd shift will start at three in the morning."

The next morning, Ty and Jack were assigned to ride with Goodnight. "Well boys, how did you like riding drag?"

Jack answered, "I thought Daddy's sawmill was dusty, but it ain't nothing compared to drag."

Ty answered. "One of the cowboys told me if you get drag two days in a row, Clint's punishing you. Don't get him mad."

Thirty

New Mexico Territory – January 1865

The herd moved north at a steady pace. Pasture for the cows was sparse. Goodnight and Clint knew the trail and that if the cattle were pushed over fifteen miles in a day, they'd lose weight.

Clint approached the men to give out the day's assignments. "Boys, today we've got to push the cows about thirty miles. I know it's too far, but we've got to do it. It's going to be a hard day. At our next campsite, we're gonna spend two days. Today, we'll make a short stop for lunch and shift assignments. Stay alert, and let's get moving."

The day was dry and cold. The sun had disappeared, and the camp was set up in the gray light before nightfall. The next morning, those on herd duty slept late. Those not on duty spent time brushing their horses and checking the horse's shoes. Several horses needed new shoes or liniment applied to swollen ankles.

At breakfast on the second morning, the night herders rushed into camp. "Clint, about ten cows were run off last night."

"How'd that happen?"

"Shorty and I were riding on opposite sides of the herd and making our rounds. We figured it took us ten minutes to make the round. Just before our relief got there, and it was getting light, I could see tracks of horses without shoes and what looks to be eight or ten cows heading east."

Goodnight listened until the cowboy finished. "Clint, I'm gonna take five men and track them down. You stay here and mind the herd. Ty, Jack, Hank, and Jim, saddle your best horse. Bring your revolvers, rifles, and extra ammo. We'll track 'em down."

Goodnight led the way, his horse at a high trot. The trail was easy to follow. As they crested a small hill, Goodnight raised his hands and halted the group. He led the men down the incline so their quarry couldn't see them. One man was assigned to hold the horses. The men crept up the hill and gazed down at the Indian camp. It was full of old women and men, children, and ten of their cows. Goodnight motioned for the men to retreat down the hill. He addressed the men, "Those poor wretches need the cows more than we do. I want to go down and talk to them. You men stay here."

As the crew crested the hill, the Indians saw them and howled in fright. Goodnight raised his hand and yelled, "Friend," and slowly walked toward them. The cowboys waited while their boss talked to a group of old men. After a short conversation and handshakes, Goodnight headed back up the hill. As their leader got to the top, he said, "Let's get back to the herd. Those poor devils escaped from Carson's death camp."

The cowboys arrived at camp just as the sun was setting. Clint asked Jack, "What happened?"

"Those Injuns were starving. Goodnight let them keep the cows."

Clint smiled and commented to Ty and Jack, "The boss growls like a bear but has a heart of gold. You'd better eat and get some sleep." He pointed west. "Those clouds look like trouble."

Thirty-One

New Mexico Territory – Early Spring 1865

Later that night, a clap of thunder and bolts of lightning woke the camp. Everyone ran to their tied-up horses and headed for the herd. No need, because the cows were heading for them. Clint yelled, "Fire shots in the air." The stampeding cows ran over two of the riders who disappeared below the dust cloud that engulfed them.

Ty and Jack turned their horses into the terrified animals. Clint raced with them and yelled, "We'll try to turn them." As they eased their horses into the cows, Clint shot the leader. The cows stumbled over the fallen animal, Ty and Jack swung their ropes, and the herd turned. Several cowboys joined them. For another half hour, the wranglers circled the animals.

Clint rode among the men. "Let them settle for a while, then we'll drive them to the river."

It took nearly an hour to return to the campsite. The cows, tired and thirsty, offered no resistance.

An exhausted group of trail hands entered the rain-soaked camp. The men lined up, and the cook served them bacon, fresh rolls, and coffee. Goodnight rode into camp, "We lost two good men this morning. After breakfast, we'll bury 'em."

The burial ceremony was short. Goodnight stared at the graves. He lifted his eyes toward heaven and said, "Lord, look kindly on these men. They did their work and never complained."

The cowboys took their turns guarding the herd. Few words were spoken.

Ty looked at Jack. "Cowboying can be worse than war. In battle, you know what's in front of you. Everything out here is unpredictable—the cows, the horses, and the weather."

"Clint told me last night he didn't like the looks of the clouds."

"We've got a lot to learn."

Clint sat next to the two friends. "You boys did right good today. And I'm sorry we lost those boys—they were good men. This country is tough. Seems like everything wants to kill you."

The men sat and sipped their coffee and stared at the campfire until it was time to sleep.

Thirty-Two

New Mexico Territory – Spring 1865

The men had been on the trail for four months. On the morning of their arrival, south of Santa Fe, Goodnight talked to the crew. "Well, it looks like we made it. Tomorrow we'll pasture the cattle about five miles south of town. Some of you only signed on till we got these cows here. After the army picks up their cows, I'm taking the rest north."

That night, Ty and Jack found Goodnight sitting by himself, looking at the mountains in the distance. Jack cleared his throat to get his attention. "Mr. Goodnight, we're fixin' to cut out as soon as you start north."

"I remember our deal. I'm leaving about five hundred cows here. Your two hundred can pasture with mine. You men have done a good job and earned your pay. What's your plan?"

Ty answered, "We'd like to find some ranch land and start our own outfit."

"You fellas' are smart enough. You've learned a lot on this drive. I've got some land over by the Palo Duro Canyon. I've been thinkin' about our first conversation. There's some land down south of a place called Quitaque. It's got good water and sits between Flat Top Mountain and Las Lingus creek. This valley is as far south as my land goes. It would be good to have you men on that land, and maybe we can work together?"

Goodnight produced a map and on it was written the JA Ranch. He explained that he and his partner had made a deal to acquire the land from the state of Texas.

Ty asked, "About how many acres are there?"

"Around ten thousand."

"How much will it cost?"

"Fifty cents an acre."

"Sir, we need a minute to talk." Goodnight nodded.

Ty and Jack moved off.

Jack scratched his head. "We'd have to come up with twenty-five hundred dollars each."

"That's right. Can you come up with your half?"

"I've saved up around five hundred dollars plus my pay for this drive."

Ty said, "I've got about seven hundred and fifty dollars saved plus the money Goodnight owes me."

They discussed the offer they'd make to Goodnight. Each man knew he'd be able to get the balance from their fathers. Ty would be their spokesman. They rejoined their boss. Ty began, "Sir, we figure that's a good offer. We'd want to give you a downpayment of one thousand dollars. We'll need our wages from this trip to buy supplies and money to live on."

Goodnight smiled. "I ain't no bank."

Ty answered, "We can raise the rest of the money from our folks."

"When can you pay the balance?"

"We have to write to our families and get banknotes transferred, probably six months from now."

"Well, that's a deal. If you don't pay me, I'll take back the land and pocket your downpayment. After we get the cattle settled, we'll get an attorney in Santa Fe to draw up the papers."

Goodnight extended his hand, first to Ty and then to Jack. "Deal. Let's get these cows bedded down." Ty and Jack declined the offered cigars.

That night Ty and Jack sat by the campfire and examined the map and discussed how to get started. Their animated conversation drew Clint's attention. "Well, y'all are excited."

Jack exclaimed, "Yes, sir. We're going to be partners and start a ranch."

In the dying embers, the men talked about their plans. Clint stood as darkness fell. "Good luck, boys. Hope we get to ride together again."

Thirty-Three

Santa Fe, New Mexico – Spring 1865

The cattle enjoyed their temporary home. Wranglers who had signed on for the drive of the reduced herd to Nebraska made camp. Jack and Ty bid farewell to the crew and headed for Santa Fe.

Ty smiled and asked Jack, "Do you think we should stay at Rancho Nambe?"

Jack smiled. "Reckon so."

The men laughed and urged their horses into a fast trot.

Ty and Jack tied their horses to the hitching post in front of Rancho Nambe. As they walked into the lobby, Oscar's concerned countenance greeted them.

Ty asked, "What's the matter?"

Oscar motioned the men to a table. "Esmeralda has been taken."

"What do you mean, taken?"

"She went north with my supply wagon to visit her tia. Some vaqueros found the wagon on the road. My men were murdered, and Esmeralda is missing."

Jack looked at Oscar. "Tia?"

Ty answered, "Aunt."

Oscar continued looking at Jack, "My daughter talked about you and how much she loved you. She was so excited to tell her tia, she begged me to let her go."

As they stared at the table, Sean O'Brien approached and pulled up a chair. "Lads, good to see you. Oscar told me what happened to the young lady. I've done some investigating. This sounds like the work of that no-good Frenchie. He and his crew took off the same time the girl went missing. We're going to get her back."

Ty asked, "How?"

"That snake is fixin to trade her to the comancheros, and I've scouted the trail. He's heading to Las Lingus Falls."

Ty and Jack jumped up. O'Brien stood. "Where are you two going?"

Jack answered. "To save Esmeralda." The men headed for the door.

O'Brien yelled. "Get back here! Y'all don't know where Las Lingus is."

Sheepishly, the two partners returned.

"There's no point running off half-cocked. We're going to plan the rescue."

Jack spoke, "Every day she's with them scoundrels, I hate to think what's happening to her."

O'Brien continued, "Frenchie knows her market price goes down if they abuse her. The rich politicians in Mexico City want undamaged goods. She'll be safe for a few days. They'll camp there until they have enough girls and boys to sell."

Ty's angered eyes scanned the group. "They're no better than slave traders. They deserve to be dead."

Thirty-Four

❖ ❖

Santa Fe, New Mexico – Spring 1865

Ty, Jack, O'Brien, and Oscar met at breakfast. They had just sat when Goodnight joined them. Oscar related the story of his daughter's disappearance. Goodnight spoke, "That crew needs to die. How can I help?"

O'Brien rubbed his chin. "We need a reason to go to Los Lingus."

Ty asked, "Where is Los Lingus?"

"It's located just off the Texas High Plains, about three hundred and fifty miles from here."

Goodnight nodded and said, "It's just north of the land you've bought from me."

O'Brien continued, "There's likely to be some Injuns and comancheros at the trading camp."

Goodnight responded, "I think we should make this look like a trading trip. We'll assemble trade goods and a small crew."

O'Brien added, "One thing on our side is that nothing will happen in the trading camp."

Jack asked, "Why's that?"

"Foul play is not allowed at the site. If Frenchie tries anything, the other traders will kill him. You might call it honor among thieves."

Goodnight could see Jack's agitation. "Put your mind to rest. The girl will not be harmed. Damaged goods don't fetch much money."

The morning was spent planning the trip and Esmeralda's rescue.

The week didn't pass quickly enough for Jack. On the morning they were due to head out, each man going on the expedition sat while O'Brien briefed them on their responsibilities. The assembled group consisted of two mules, a transport driven by a mountain man, and Woody's chuck wagon. Each man had a spare horse, two revolvers, and a rifle. The train headed out, with O'Brien and Goodnight in the lead. Jack, Ty, Clint, and a cowboy herded the horses, and the others followed.

That day they traveled fifty miles. At camp, Woody prepared one of his specialties. The men gathered around and ate. O'Brien had each man recite his rescue duties.

The trail followed a green valley through the New Mexico territory. The path to the High Plains passed through a valley and onto a rolling, grass-filled plain populated with elk and antelope. The camp on the third night was next to a water-filled playa lake.

At sunset, the travelers could hear wolves howling in the distance. That night, O'Brien took extra precautions. The horses could graze for an hour and drink their fill of water. They were hobbled and tied to a high line stretched between the wagons.

When their meal was finished, Woody gathered all the uneaten food. The food scraps were taken on the other side of the lake, and poisoned deer meat marked the spot. That night, howls and growls filled the air. Around midnight, the wolves' racket stopped.

After breakfast, O'Brien had the men and the cargo wagon follow him around the lake. Jack spoke, "Look at all those dead critters."

O'Brien dismounted. "Okay boys, let's get busy. We'll have wolf pelts to trade. You boys watch me."

Ty and Jack spent the morning skinning wolves.

The grass on the trail suddenly ended, and the party stopped at the base of a three-hundred-foot escarpment. They followed a well-worn switchback trail up the steep wall. As a precaution, the cowboys flanked the wagons and tied on their lines. The horses strained, and the cowboys dallied their ropes and helped pull.

At the top, the High Plains disappeared over the eastern horizon. Camp was set up, and the horses were hobbled and allowed to graze.

Goodnight and O'Brien gathered the party.

Goodnight started. "We're about a hundred miles from Los Lingus. We're going to move fast. I want to be in place by the day after tomorrow. We'll split up. Ty and Jack will go with O'Brien and the trade goods and mules to the trading site."

O'Brien added, "Everyone knows his job, but let's go over it one more time."

The next day the group split. O'Brien and his crew headed out first. Goodnight yelled, "Be careful!"

O'Brien responded, "Watch your back, Charley."

Woody and Clint laughed.

Goodnight growled, "I was riding this range while you were still playing bagpipes." He bellowed at his crew, "Get ready, we're burnin' daylight." And he turned his back to tighten his horse's saddle cinch.

"Okay, Charley."

Goodnight spun around. "Who said that?"

Thirty-Five

Palo Duro Canyon – June 1865

O'Brien's party followed the trail across the flat plain. After about fifty miles, the landscape changed. They made camp early. O'Brien said to Ty and Jack, "Let's take a little ride. Fred will watch over the camp." Fred nodded. He was a man of few words.

The men rode about two miles. Ty exclaimed, "Look at that!" A vast canyon lay at their feet.

O'Brien pointed. "This is Palo Duro Canyon. It goes about a hundred miles south and east. These canyons are as rough as a cob. The Indians call them the breaks. In the morning, we'll follow the canyon to Los Lingus."

Jack spoke, "I ain't never seen anything so beautiful. Look at that orange and red rock and the white lines running through it. That stream looks like it flows down the middle."

"The red and orange rocks are hardened clay, and the white stripes are limestone. At the bottom of the canyon is where the Comanche make their winter camp. That gray-looking clay is caliche, which added to gravel and sand makes good materials for a dugout."

"Wow, that's got to be seven or eight hundred feet down. We've got mountains in the Catskills but nothing like this."

Ty pointed across the canyon, "What's that rim at the top?"

"It's called caprock. It surrounds the canyon and it's solid granite. Tomorrow, we'll go down there and follow the canyon until we get to Los Lingus."

Rising in the gray light before dawn, the men ate a breakfast of dried biscuits and jerky. Each man led a pack mule carrying trade goods. The party rode to the edge of the canyon.

Jack asked, "How do we get down?"

O'Brien chuckled. "Follow me. You'll see."

O'Brien led them along the ridge for about a mile and stopped. "See that break in the caprock? Below it is a trail that leads to the bottom."

Ty looked at Jack. "We're not riding billy goats."

O'Brien cautioned, "Get your horse's nose pointed down the trail. Don't try to guide him and he'll figure it out, same with the mule. Now keep quiet and follow me."

They lined up behind O'Brien, and Fred brought up the rear.

Thirty-Six

❖ ··◆··❖··◆·· ❖

Los Lingus – June 1865

The switchback trail down the canyon wall was no trip for the faint of heart. As the party followed O'Brien and eased its way down the steep path, the horses and mules needed no direction. Their instincts guided them.

Once at the bottom, O'Brien dismounted. "We did that right handy. That's an old Indian trail. If someone didn't show you where it is, you'd never find it. I've seen cavalry race up and down the rim, trying to figure out how the Indians disappeared." He loosened the cinch strap. "We'll let the horses eat some grass and drink. I want to be near Los Lingus before we make camp."

The men followed streambeds and game trails south. O'Brien set a fast pace. Obstacles meant nothing to the old mountain man. The valley's width varied from two miles to eight, and the soaring cliffs with layers of red and orange clay met the granite caprock eight hundred feet above the travelers.

They startled several deer and watched them bound away. The natural beauty of the canyon was hypnotic.

O'Brien yelled, "Watch out for rattlesnakes sunning themselves on the trail." He chuckled, "They get mad when you step on them."

The deep breaks challenged their riding skills, and the mesquite thorns tore at arms and legs. Jack remarked, "I've been in rough country, but this beats all."

O'Brien halted. "We'll dry camp here. No fires. We're about ten miles from Los Lingus. I want to get there by mid-morning." They camped near a stream. The horses and mules drank and grazed. Each animal received half a sack of feed before being high-lined for the night. "We need to keep the stock in good shape. Never know when we're going to have to run for it."

The men spent the next hour going over the next day's plan.

Ty asked, "Any idea how many of Frenchie's men will be with him?"

"He usually runs with six or eight."

Jack added, "We killed one of his men trying to steal horses outside Santa Fe."

"Anyone riding with that scoundrel deserves what he got."

The next morning after a sparse breakfast of cold beans and dried biscuits, the rescuers got underway. As they approached the Los Lingus River, O'Brien commented, "Remember what I told you."

They followed the river west for a mile, then O'Brien raised his hand and waved at a gunman perched on top of a small bluff.

"That you, O'Brien?"

"Who else has my beautiful head of hair?"

"What's your business?"

"We've come to trade for beaver pelts and buffalo hides."

"There's some Indians with pelts and Frenchie has horses and cows."

The trail followed the river for another half mile to its source. Water cascaded down a red cliff into a pool and overflowed into the streambed. The land around the stream was cleared by years of use. Several campsites nestled under the shade of the cottonwood trees. A cool breeze made its way down the cliff.

O'Brien cautioned his partners, "Keep your eyes open and your mouth shut. We'll make camp and spread out our trade goods."

They established their camp. The trade goods were arranged around the site. Several groups of comancheros drifted over to inspect their wares. The Indian traders recognized O'Brien. Conversations were carried out in sign language.

Several trades were completed. Jack and Ty were kept busy sorting and stacking furs, carrying buckets of water and feed to their animals, and erecting a lean-to.

The partners paid attention to the sign language. Jack remarked, "Knowing how to sign could come in handy." Ty nodded in agreement.

Thirty-Seven

Los Lingus Camp – June 1865

A familiar face appeared. "Bonjour, O'Brien."

"Don't speak that frog language at me, Frenchie, I don't understand it."

Frenchie's blackened teeth filled his smirking face. He turned to the men accompanying him. "Je vais nos fourrures après que Je te coupe la gorge." He continued in English, "You've come to trade for furs. What's the matter? Couldn't find Indians to cheat in the mountains?"

O'Brien answered. "What brings you and your cutthroats to Los Lingus?"

"We have horses and cows up on the plains to trade."

O'Brien picked up a fur pelt. "I've heard that you have women to trade."

"Those women are headed south with us and have been promised to rich Mexicans. They're too fine for trappers. You couldn't afford them."

"There's no sense talking."

"Au revoir. That means till we meet again." Frenchie and his men walked away.

Jack asked, "I wonder what he said?" O'Brien smiled. "Those furs will be mine after I cut your throat."

Ty commented, "A fair translation."

O'Brien scratched his head. "I didn't want him to know I understood French." He looked at Ty, "I didn't think black men could speak French. I guess we're both surprised."

Ty responded, "Vous ne connaissez pas beaucoup d'hommes noirs de la Louisiane?"

O'Brien smiled, "You're correct. I don't know many black people from Louisiana."

Jack was confused. "What are you two talking about?"

Ty said, "You got the gist of it. Frenchie is taking our bait."

The day's trading continued. That night they cooked a meal of desiccated vegetables and deer meat.

Jack asked, "What did the Confederates call those vegetables?"

"Defecated vegetables."

Ty smiled. "Same as us."

O'Brien smirked. "Those dried vegetables have gotten me through a lot of hard winters. Now eat and get some sleep, because tomorrow's gonna be busy." Fred nodded in agreement.

The next morning, O'Brien said, "Let's have a good breakfast, then pack up and leave."

The quartet headed down the river trail. At the junction of the river and canyon trails, they turned south. As they crested a hill, they could see their destination. Three peaks dominated the horizon—two formed points, and the one in the middle was a flat top.

O'Brien motioned and said, "That's where we're goin'. Let's pick up speed and get to tonight's camp." They spurred their horses, and the mules kept pace. The land around the mountains was a rolling plain. Across another small river and up and down through steep canyons, they arrived at the campsite late in the day.

As they dismounted, Ty remarked, "I haven't seen hide nor hair of Goodnight and the others."

O'Brien smiled. "Don't worry. He's been watching us for the last hour."

The sun was sinking. "No time to waste. Let's get the animals watered and fed." The men quickly unsaddled the horses and mules. Between two large cottonwood trees, they strung a high line.

They dug a firepit and lined it with rocks. Ty and Jack gathered wood while O'Brien and Fred unpacked the deer meat and dried vegetables. "Well, boys, let's brew coffee. If Frenchie and his men can't follow our trail, they'll find us by following their noses."

With the meal finished, the men laid out their bedrolls and threw more wood on the fire.

Thirty-Eight

Flat Top Mountain – Summer 1865

Frenchie and his gang picked up O'Brien's trail at midday. Frenchie remarked, "They'll camp near the stream by the Flat Top Mountain. They're going to the Comanche camp in Blanco Canyon."

On the escarpment above their intended victims' camp, they dismounted. One man was detailed to watch the horses. Frenchie and five of his gang carefully descended on the sleeping travelers. The ambushers spread out around the bedrolls. Frenchie yelled, "Fire, kill them all." As the crew aimed their pistols and rifles, the valley erupted in gunfire. On the first volley, half of the cutthroats fell, and another volley ended the battle.

Two of the culprits moaned as a shot rang out above them on the escarpment. Goodnight walked out of the thick brush. "I think we've got 'em all. Sounds like old Woody got his man."

Clint mused, "Last time I'll insult his cooking."

O'Brien walked over to one of the moaning men. "Looks like we didn't finish Frenchie." He squatted next to him. "Well, I guess you didn't get to slit my throat." The wounded desperado spit at him. O'Brien continued, "You've scalped a lot of decent folks. It's time for you to find out how it feels." O'Brien grabbed a handful of greasy hair and with his knife, cut just below Frenchie's hairline. The screams echoed through the canyon. He wiped his blade on his victim's shirt and worked his hand into the cut he'd made, and once he had enough leverage, he pulled the scalp until all that was visible was the skull bone. O'Brien pulled the scalp to the back of Frenchie's head and severed the scalp from the head. "Now Frenchie, that weren't so bad."

The Frenchman whimpered. "Shoot me."

O'Brien stood. Ty and Jack looked shocked. "Boys, after an Injun scalps someone, they hang them upside down over a fire and let them die slowly. Frenchie figured that was gonna happen to him." He thought for a minute, "If you're ever about to be caught by Injuns, use your last bullet on yourself." He pointed his pistol at Frenchie's head. The shot reverberated down the canyon.

The men hobbled and tied their horses and mules to the high line.

Goodnight said, "We've got to bury these dead men, or we'll have wolves with us all night." It took about an hour to bury the bodies. Their work complete, the crew spread out their bedrolls.

O'Brien stated, "You boys get some sleep."

Jack lay in his bedroll, unable to sleep.

Ty yawned and asked, "What's bothering you?"

"Thinking about Esmeralda."

"Worrying won't get it done. Go to sleep."

Thirty-Nine

Above Los Lingus – Summer 1865

As he opened his eyes, Jack shouted, "We've got to go rescue Esmeralda!"

Goodnight smiled. "That's what we're planning to do." He continued, "On our way across the top of the caprock, we ran into Frenchie's stock and prisoners. They're about a half-mile back from Los Lingus, and only two guards are with them."

O'Brien spoke. "We'll take only our horses. I've got an idea."

The six men rode at a fast trot. As they approached the camp, O'Brien called out, "Spanish Joe, is that you?"

"Sí, O'Brien, what you doin' here?"

"I made a deal with Frenchie for the cattle. He said you'd help me sort out ten head."

"Well, I think I have to check with the boss."

Another vaquero rode up. "Que pasa?"

Goodnight and the other men drew their pistols. "If you boys want to see home again, unholster your pistols and hand them over."

The two men handed their weapons to Goodnight.

Ty asked, "Where are the women? Talk now if you want to live."

Spanish Joe stammered and pointed. "En una pequeña cueva de esa manera."

Ty translated and pointed. "In a small cave, that way."

Goodnight said, "You two go and find the girl. We'll hold these two until you return." He looked at the Mexicans, and in Spanish said, "You better be telling the truth." The cowboys tied the captives' arms behind them. Goodnight stated, "Sentar." The crestfallen youngsters slumped to the ground.

Forty

Rescue at Los Lingus – Summer 1865

Ty and Jack rode to the edge of the caprock. The trail down was easy to see. They dismounted and walked down the path. A short walk brought them to an overhang. The partners were shocked to find two women bound, hand and foot, with gags in their mouths.

Jack ran to Esmeralda and gently cut her bindings and removed her gag. "By God, I've found you. I ain't never gonna leave your side again."

Esmeralda cried, "Mi amor." Jack's arms wrapped around her.

The other woman, in Indian dress, cringed as Ty approached. He held up his hands as a sign of peace. His soothing and rudimentary sign language removed the fear from her eyes. Ty slowly took his knife and cut the bindings. He handed her his canteen, she drank half and returned it to him. Relaxed, her radiant smile warmed Ty's heart.

It was fortunate that Ty had observed O'Brien and picked up the basics of sign language. The young girl massaged her wrists and feet. Ty signed, "My name," and in a gentle voice said, "Ty."

The young woman stroked her long, raven hair and pointed to herself, "Topsannah."

"I don't understand what that means, but you sure are pretty." His face broadened into a smile.

Topsannah smiled. "Habla español?"

Ty responded, "Sí."

They continued talking in Spanish. Ty asked, "How did you get captured?"

"I was gathering plums and wandered too far from camp. The bandits jumped me and brought me here. My tribe is the Quohadas."

"That sounds like the name of a man I met—his name is Quanah Parker."

"Quanah Parker is my brother."

"What does Topsannah mean?"

"Prairie Flower."

Ty pointed at her. "Flor." He paused, "In English, that means flower." He motioned the woman to follow him as he exited their prison.

The party rested at the crest. Jack questioned the ladies, "Did any of the men abuse you?"

Esmeralda and Flower conferred out of earshot of Ty and Jack. Esmeralda spoke, "If that had happened, we would have killed ourselves before we'd let those animals touch us."

The look of defiance convinced the men they meant what they said. She softened and said, "Those two Mexican boys treated us like ladies. They said if they ever get away from this gang of murderers, they'd go home and never leave again."

The men mounted and held their hands out to the women.

Esmeralda frowned. "I'm dirty."

Jack replied, "You look good to me. When we get to camp, you can clean up in the stream."

Flower tried to shake her head no. Ty grabbed her arm and pulled her up behind him. Flower relaxed as her arms embraced him.

Esmeralda leaned her head on Jack's shoulder. Her tears fell down his back.

Ty said with a smile, "Let's get back to the others."

Jack nodded. "We've had a good day."

Forty-One

Los Lingus – Summer 1865

The rescue party arrived to find Goodnight and O'Brien glaring at the prisoners. The men helped the women down. Goodnight remarked, "That's Quanah Parker's little sister."

O'Brien said, "You two have a talent for saving important Comanches."

Esmeralda could see the look of terror on the faces of the two young Mexicans. She motioned Goodnight and O'Brien to follow her. After they were out of earshot, she began, "Those two young men did not harm us. Each day they made sure we had enough to eat and drink. They never intruded on our privacy. What got them involved with those cutthroats, I don't know. They don't deserve to die."

Goodnight and O'Brien walked up to the young Mexicans. Goodnight looked at Spanish Joe and the vaquero and in Spanish said, "You boys come from good families. Frenchie and the rest of the crew are dead." Goodnight continued, "Your compadre, José's son, is dead, and I had to tell his father. Valdez asked me not to kill you." He pointed his finger at the duo. "If I ever see you again north of the border, I'll hang you."

The two could take their horses and weapons plus an old pack mule with a supply of food and water. They mounted their horses, and Goodnight said, "Ve ahora."

Jack asked Ty, "What did he tell those Mexicans?"

"Go now."

Forty-Two

Flat Top Mountain – Summer 1865

The group followed the trail back to the Flat Top Mountain campsite. Goodnight and O'Brien led the way. Esmeralda and Flower rode horses and enjoyed the ride. The cowboys herded the captured livestock while the mountain men led the mules. Ty and Jack trailed the group with the rescued women.

Goodnight halted. "We're above the camp. The livestock can graze, and after a while, we'll herd them down to the stream for water. You cowboys, take the first shift. We'll relieve you in two hours." The animals relaxed and grazed.

The other group headed down off the caprock, following a game trail to the campsite. The horses were unsaddled, hobbled, and turned out to graze. O'Brien pointed to a path that disappeared into the brush next to the stream and addressed Ty and Jack, "Escort the women down the trail, and you'll find a natural shower." He smiled at the women and handed them a wrapped-up bundle of pants and shirts. "Here's some clean clothes and soap."

The four young people followed the trail through a thicket of vines, which widened into a cliff-sheltered valley. A cool breeze filled the air with the smell of cedar. About a hundred yards in, a waterfall cascaded between layers of red clay and sandstone into a pool of water, making a natural bathtub. Ty commented, "Look at those ferns. There's water dripping out of the rock."

Jack stepped closer. "This must be an aquifer. I've seen small ones back home, but nothing like this."

Esmeralda smiled and said, "This is perfecto. You men head back to camp, and we'll join you in a little while—and no peeking."

The men laughed and headed back to camp.

O'Brien and Goodnight sat talking. The mountain men busied themselves gathering wood and making a fire. Goodnight said to Ty and Jack, "You boys help get the camp set up. We've got to figure out our next step."

Without comment, Ty and Jack gathered cedar limbs and constructed a lean-to. "This should do the ladies right fine."

They gathered rocks from a nearby hillside and constructed a firepit. Ty motioned toward Goodnight and O'Brien. "Let's go see what they are talking about."

Goodnight motioned and said to them, "Pull up a log and sit. We think we figured out our next step."

O'Brien spoke, "That girl you're calling Flower is a Commanche. I know the location of her village. I'll take her back. Fred and I will take the pack mules with us to her village. You boys, Goodnight, and the cowboys will take the Mexican girl to Santa Fe."

Ty spoke up, looking at O'Brien, "I want to go with you."

O'Brien's lip curled. "You can come if you want, but we plan to spend a couple of months trading and trapping."

Jack responded, "Ty and I have got to talk about this. Our cows are at Santa Fe, and we have to settle up with Mr. Goodnight."

Goodnight frowned. "This here land is where your ranch is going to be."

Jack looked at Ty. "We need to sit and talk this out."

Flower and Esmeralda made their way back to camp.

Jack commented, "It took you gals almost two hours." A grin betrayed his make-believe anger. "Looks like it was worth the wait."

The women had washed and dried their clothes. Flower's raven hair glistened. Esmeralda's riding clothes clung to her body. Jack stated, "Y'all clean up good." Ty kicked him.

Esmeralda handed O'Brien the bundle he had given them. "We wore your clothes until ours were dry. Thank you."

While waiting, the mountain men prepared a meal. They boiled the dried vegetables and roasted venison. The smell of coffee filled the air.

Esmeralda smiled, "Muy bien."

After the meal, the women gathered the dishes, cups, and silverware and went to the stream to wash them.

Ty glanced at Goodnight, "We need to talk to you."

"Talk?"

Ty and Jack explained that the money for the land would be deposited in his account in Santa Fe within the month. The partners had set this up already. They had much to do, and Ty asked, "Is it okay if we keep our cows on your place in Santa Fe until next spring?"

"That's fine. In the spring we can drive your cows and mine to the top of Palo Duro."

Jack responded, "I'm going to go with you back to Santa Fe. Ty wants to tag along with O'Brien. We plan to meet up to drive the cows here after the winter."

"That'll work. You men help me get my cows to Palo Duro, and I'll help you drive your cows here."

Forty-Three

Partners Head in Different Directions – Fall 1865

Ty and Jack rose early. Woody prepared a breakfast of Dutch-oven biscuits, bacon, grease gravy, and coffee. Flower and Esmeralda went to the stream to clean the utensils. The partners sat with Goodnight and O'Brien. O'Brien asked, "Ty, are you sure you want to come with me to the Comanche camp?"

Ty nodded and said, "I'd like to learn more about trading with the Indians since they'll be our neighbors."

"Are you sure you don't want to learn more about Flower?"

Jack and Goodnight exploded in laughter. Goodnight exclaimed, "We've seen how you look at her."

"Jack's fixin' to get a wife. Maybe—I'm tired of being around all y'all's ugly faces."

"Can't disagree with you."

The women returned and packed. O'Brien asked Flower in Comanche, "The black man wants to come with us to your camp. Would you like that?"

Flower nodded and said, "Haa."

Ty asked, "What did you say?"

"I asked her if she thought she'd like to be your wife. You heard her answer. She laughed."

Goodnight chuckled, "He's joshing you. He asked her if she'd like to have you come to her people's camp. 'Haa' means yes."

Ty and Flower exchanged smiles.

Goodnight remarked, "Ain't love grand."

With all the horses saddled and the mules packed, the group rode out of the valley to the top of the caprock.

Jack and Ty had agreed on a plan. Jack would spend the winter in Santa Fe, looking after their cattle. Ty explained that he was attracted to Flower and wanted to see what would develop.

Ty remarked, "I thought you were gonna talk to Esmeralda's father?"

Jack answered, "I am."

"What makes you think he'll let his daughter marry a gringo?"

"You think Quanah is going to approve of Flower marrying a black man?"

"I guess we both have some finding out to do."

The party reached the top of the escarpment. O'Brien, Ty, Flower, and the two mountain men leading the mules headed to Blanco Canyon. Goodnight's party of Jack, Esmeralda, and the cowboys driving the livestock struck out for Santa Fe. As they separated, Jack held up his hand. Ty said, "See you in the spring."

Forty-Four

―――――◆◆◆――――◆◆◆◆――――――――◆◆――――

Blanco Canyon – Fall 1865

O'Brien led the way to Blanco Canyon. The trail followed the ridge of the escarpment. The level plains stretched south and west. A light breeze blew, cooling the travelers. A stand of brown-tipped cedar trees swayed in the breeze. A molting mist of pollen sprang from the branches, bathing the party in a cloud of fine dust. Ty rubbed his nose and sneezed. O'Brien laughed and said, "Welcome to the canyons."

The trail the party followed skirted canyons filled with cottonwood trees, cedar, and mesquite bushes broken up by aquifer-fed streams. The contrast between the flat plains and the bucolic canyon amazed Ty.

Ty and Flower rode together, with O'Brien and the mountain men leading the way. At a lunchtime rest stop, O'Brien commented, "We'll be at Quanah's camp before nightfall."

Ty remarked, "I ain't never seen land like this before."

O'Brien said, "The Spanish named these plains 'Llano Estacado.'"

Ty translated. "Land of stakes."

Flower smiled and said, "My people were here before the Spaniards. This land is where the buffalo graze."

In the early afternoon, the party reached a place where the canyon widened. O'Brien stopped his horse. "Ty, this is the beginning of Blanco Canyon. Once we head down, there's no turning back."

Ty responded, "What are we waiting for?"

The trail to the valley floor was steep but nothing the horses and mules couldn't handle. At the bottom, the party followed a path west along the riverbank, the brush beat back by years of use. The party rounded a curve and confronted a group of ten Comanche warriors. O'Brien held up his hand and spoke in Comanche, "We've come to trade and bring Quanah's sister Topsannah to her people." O'Brien whispered to Ty, "Let me do the talking."

The leader of the warriors rode to Flower's side and let out a yell of joy. The warriors raised their coup sticks and spears in a salute. Their joyful yelps brought smiles to the faces of the trappers. The leader motioned O'Brien to follow him.

≪•◆◆•≫

The traders followed the warriors. The canyon widened. Ty noted, "It would be hard to find this place if you didn't know where you were going."

O'Brien smirked. "The U.S. cavalry has been trying to find this camp for years."

Teepees straddled the river. Rough streets traversed the camp, with a giant teepee dominating its center. O'Brien noted, "That big tent will be Quanah Parker's." The party rode through the encampment followed by an ever-growing crowd of warriors, women, children, and dogs. In front of Quanah's teepee was a large clearing with a firepit in the center. A mile downstream, bluffs surrounded the canyon, forming a natural barrier. A herd of horses grazed at the foot of the rock walls under the watchful eyes of Indian guards.

The group stopped. Quanah approached them, wearing his ceremonial headdress. "O'Brien, welcome to our camp. I see you've brought my little sister home."

"We caught up with Frenchie and convinced him to release her." O'Brien removed the scalp from his saddlebag and tossed it to the ground at Quanah's feet.

"Looks like he agreed to lend you his hair."

"Thought you might use it to decorate your coup stick."

Quanah looked at his sister, saying, "Go visit with your aunt. We'll talk later."

Topsannah approached an old Indian woman, whose face creased into a smile. The woman took her hand and led her away. The crowd broke up, the women went back to work, and the men lounged in their favorite spots.

The group dismounted. Quanah motioned for the men to follow him into his tent. The tent stood ten feet at the center, with a rope hung from the crossed poles at the top and held in place by a stake driven into the ground. O'Brien sat next to the chief, and Ty and the two mountain men spread out around the perimeter of the tent. Quanah spoke first. "I see you have trade goods on your mules."

"I plan to camp nearby and trade for furs."

Quanah answered, "Make your camp a half a mile north. You'll not be bothered. Trading can start tomorrow."

Forty-Five

Blanco Canyon – Fall 1865

O'Brien led the party to a site near the east wall of the escarpment. The campsite was clear and near the river. It took the men the balance of the day to set up camp. Preparation began for their evening meal. Seated around the campfire, O'Brien stated, "Tomorrow, we'll spread out our trade goods."

Ty asked, "Is it okay if I visit Flower?"

"No. Until Quanah gives his permission, stay clear."

"I'd like to marry her and start a ranch."

"In due time, laddie."

The night was clear. Stars filled the sky. In the distance came the sound of a drumbeat.

The mountain men and O'Brien talked about tomorrow's trade. Ty interrupted, "What's going on?"

"The Injuns are celebrating Flower's return. They'll dance all night. When the celebration is over, the chiefs and senior warriors will talk about what to do with us. Not all the young warriors are happy about us being here."

One of the mountain men added, "We've traded with the Comanches for a long time but now that the Civil War is almost over, the cavalry has a new mission—protecting the new settlers. Many braves have died." He stopped and looked at O'Brien.

"We've been friends to the Indians and trading partners. I hope that the old men convince the young ones that we mean them no harm. Tomorrow we'll spread out our trade goods and keep our best horses saddled, in case we have to make a hasty retreat."

The next morning, they rekindled the cooking fire, made coffee and breakfast, and ate. The group spread their trade goods out on buffalo hides. Pots, pans, knives, and beads were arranged for the expected business. Each man saddled his best horse and loaded his saddlebag with supplies, just in case.

The first to arrive was Quanah, and Flower walked a short distance behind. Quanah picked up a knife. "How many hides for this?"

O'Brien winked at Ty and turned to Quanah. "Three beavers."

Quanah dropped the knife. "Too much," and walked away.

Flower smiled at Ty and followed her brother.

After Quanah was out of earshot, O'Brien looked at Ty. "We get to keep our hair."

The day was busy. Indians made their way to the traders' camp. Ty was kept busy serving coffee and tending to the livestock. It also allowed him to study sign language.

Quanah sent word that the group was invited to eat with him that night.

Forty-Six

Blanco Canyon – Fall 1865

The sun was beginning its journey into the western edge of the canyon. The men packed their trade goods and left the newly acquired pelts hidden in a cliff alcove, and covered the site with cedar branches.

O'Brien stated, "Time to go, lads, don't want to be late for dinner."

The men headed to Quanah's teepee. The flap was pulled back, indicating that it was alright to enter.

Quanah stood and pointed at the buffalo hides spread around. He motioned the men to sit. O'Brien began the conversation in sign language. "We've been friends for many moons. I'm troubled. The war between the blue and gray has ended."

Quanah signed, "Who won?"

"The blue won the last battle and the gray soldiers have headed home."

Quanah stroked his long braid. "The grays tried to get the Comanche to fight with them against blues. We thought it was a bad idea to take sides. My people heard what happened to the Navajo. I should have killed Carson at Adobe Walls."

O'Brien shook his head. "Goodnight told me the Navajos were being taken to Bosque Redondo. That's a death sentence."

"The time of the Indian is passing. I'll fight until the people agree with me."

O'Brien responded, "I don't understand?"

"The young warriors think the white man can be defeated." Quanah shook his head, "It's not possible."

Several women entered the teepee with bowls of food and chunks of meat. Flower set the food in front of Ty and smiled.

Quanah looked at Ty. "My sister told me of your kindness to her."

Ty's eyes sparkled. "She's a good woman, strong and smart."

"You and your partner, Jack, told me of your plan to start a ranch."

"That's our plan. We want to settle in the land between the Llano Estacado and the Flat Top Mountain."

Quanah answered using a mixture of sign language and English. "Goodnight wants to settle in Palo Duro Canyon. He's been chasing Indians and fighting the blue soldiers for a long time. He knows to stay away from me. When he was with the Texas Rangers, he killed my father and stole my mother. They captured a young girl and thought it was Topsannah, but my mother hid her when the Rangers attacked."

When the meal was over, Quanah said, "The evening dance is about to begin. Time for you to go back to your camp. Our young warriors get worked up." Looking at Ty, he said, "They think you're a buffalo soldier."

O'Brien placed his finger on his lips and motioned for the group to leave.

The next morning, as they set up for another day of trading, O'Brien mentioned to Ty. "It looks like you've made a good impression."

"I don't understand."

"Allowing his sister to serve you is a sign that he approves of you."

"What should I do next?"

"Nothing." O'Brien and the mountain men shared a good laugh. Then he said, "We'll trade for a while longer. Before we leave, you'll have to get Quanah's permission and make sure the girl agrees. You might be challenged by a young buck. Don't start the fight but make sure you finish it."

Forty-Seven

Blanco Canyon – Late Fall 1865

The next morning, Quanah walked into camp and nodded to Ty. "Tomorrow we hunt buffalo. Bring your spotted horse." He turned and headed back to his village.

Ty looked at O'Brien. "What was that all about?"

"I think Quanah wants to see how you handle yourself."

Ty was busy saddling his horse. O'Brien rode up. "I'm coming with you. The other boys will do the trading today. Do you think that spotted horse can keep up?"

Ty spurred his horse. "We'll see."

In front of Quanah's teepee, ten warriors sat on their best horses. A muscled stud horse stood tied to a post. Each horse's tail was braided with colorful markings, and each reflected the rider's taste. Ty and O'Brien reined their horses near the hunting party. Several warriors gave Ty a wary glance. Quanah, followed by Flower and his wife, exited the teepee. Quanah mounted his horse, and his wife approached and added a white lightning bolt to the stud's flank. Flower approached Ty's horse and drew a white circle on the horse's neck. The younger warriors scowled. O'Brien leaned over and whispered to Ty. "Keep your eye on those young bucks."

Quanah urged his horse forward. The hunting party followed. The horsemen followed Quanah up a narrow trail to the top of the caprock. Two of the older Indians trotted ahead of the group. The others followed at a slow trot. The green grass stretched to the horizon. The plains appeared featureless, but close inspection proved otherwise. The group rode past depressions filled with water. O'Brien explained to Ty, "The Spanish named these playa lakes. Some think the buffaloes hollowed out the ground, and others think they're natural depressions. This is a good sign. The buffs need to drink."

The depression was surrounded by short hills. As the party crested the hill, all stopped. The two scouts, in sign language, told that a small herd of about one hundred buffaloes had gathered two miles ahead. Quanah indicated that the hunting party would split into three groups. The trackers would stay in place until the two groups were in position on the flanks of the herd.

Ty and O'Brien followed Quanah and another hunter. They rode at a trot south, and the other group headed west. After two miles, Quanah halted the men and indicated they should spread out and head toward the buffaloes.

O'Brien pulled his rifle from its scabbard. Ty held his weapon in his right hand, balanced on his leg. The party reached the top of a hill, and the buffalo herd was before them. The other group sat opposite them as the two scouts approached from the rear and gave bloodcurdling yells.

Quanah urged his horse into a canter. O'Brien said, "Okay, laddie, here we go."

The buffaloes stampeded as the three groups converged on the herd. Quanah was the first to down a big bull with a thrust of his hunting lance. Ty dropped another massive male with a shot through the head. The chase lasted about ten minutes. Behind the hunters lay twelve dead buffaloes. The dead animals were large bulls or old cows. Quanah raised his hand, bringing the hunters to a halt.

Ty said, "That was fun." He patted his horse, "You did well." O'Brien rode up, and Ty smiled and looked at the mountain man. "I've never seen such a display of horsemanship."

O'Brien agreed, "The Comanches are the finest horsemen in the west. One on one, the cavalry wouldn't stand a chance. When I first met Quanah, his group totaled over a thousand braves."

"Did the army kill them?"

"They killed some, but what really did them in was smallpox and measles."

The other members of the hunting party gathered around Quanah. In the distance, Ty spotted a caravan of Indians leading horses with travoises lashed to their backs. Each man rode to the animal he'd brought down and waited for his family to bring the pack horses. Skinning took about two hours. Flower and her sister-in-law worked on Quanah's catch. Ty and O'Brien rendered their harvest ready for transport.

Members of the hunting party rode by and nodded at Ty and O'Brien. "Looks like you passed the test."

"Well laddie, time to pack the meat." O'Brien cut along the buffalo's underbelly and removed the dead animal's liver.

With that, O'Brien handed Ty the warm liver from the dead buffalo, "Here, take a bite, you'll like it."

Ty cut off a piece and tentatively bit into it. "Not bad."

With the work finished, the hunting party walked their horses back to Blanco Canyon for a night of celebration.

As Ty enjoyed the peaceful walk across the plains, he thought, *I wonder what Jack's doing?*

Forty-Eight

New Mexico Territory – Fall 1865

Jack and Esmeralda rode together as they headed for Santa Fe. Esmeralda asked, "Why did Ty go with O'Brien?"

"I think he's taken a fancy to Flower."

"We spent several weeks together; she's nice. She told me her brother, Quanah, knows that their way of life is doomed. Her mother, a white woman, was captured by the Texas Rangers and taken away. Flower managed to hide, and the Rangers took another girl they thought was her. The girl was simple-minded, and Mrs. Parker never corrected the Rangers' mistake."

"I know Ty is attracted to her."

The party followed Goodnight as they skirted the canyons. The sight of the endless grass contrasted with the rough brush and tree-lined canyons. That night, the party made its way down the canyon wall and set up camp next to a stream and a plum thicket. Enormous cottonwood trees sheltered the party. The horses and mules were hobbled and allowed to graze. Once the camp was set up, Goodnight said, "Why don't you two go and gather some plums, and we'll have dessert tonight."

Jack and Esmeralda were picking plums, and suddenly Esmeralda shrieked and jumped away from the bushes. "Serpienta!" The rattlesnake lunged and grazed her leg. Jack picked up a rock and crushed its head.

"Oh, my God." Jack picked her up and ran to camp.

"She's been bitten by a rattlesnake."

Goodnight spread out a blanket. "Put her down." He immediately went to work inspecting the wound. "I don't think the snake got its fangs set." He called out, "Anyone chewing tobacco?"

Esmeralda held up her hand, "Por favor deje de."

Goodnight translated, "She asked us to please stop."

Esmeralda smiled and continued in English. She pointed at Jack's knife. "Is that knife sharp?"

"Yes."

"Hand it to me, please." Jack was puzzled but handed her his knife.

She tested it with her finger and asked, "Does anyone have some whiskey?"

Woody nodded sheepishly.

"May I have some?"

Woody dug through his saddlebag and retrieved a flask and handed it to the girl.

"Gracias." She poured the alcohol across the blade and gulped a mouthful. Without hesitation she cut an X over the rattlesnake bite and squeezed the wound. It bled until she was satisfied, then she dried the wound. She smiled at the cowboy and held out her hand. "The tobacco, please." She spread the brown glob on the wound and bound it with a clean rag.

The men stared in disbelief. Goodnight commented, "She's a keeper. We're in a good place to camp." He looked at Jack, "Go fetch her saddle. She should keep her head elevated. I don't think the bite is deep, but we'll see how it looks in the morning."

Jack spent the night at Esmeralda's side. The morning brought good news. Esmeralda woke and looked at Jack. "I'm alright. Feeling a little dizzy and hungry."

Goodnight squatted next to her and placed his hand on her forehead. "A little fever but not bad. We'll spend another day here and see how you are tomorrow."

Esmeralda stated, "I'm good, let's get going."

Goodnight shook his head. "No. You need to rest, and we need some fresh meat. The boys and I are goin' hunting. Jack will keep you company."

With that, Goodnight stood. "Well, let's get started, time's a-wastin'."

By mid-afternoon, the hunting party returned with a gutted deer tied on the back of a mule. Woody asked, "Have y'all ever tasted deer camp tenderloin?" Jack and Esmeralda shook their heads. "You're in for a treat."

Goodnight and the cowboys took about an hour to skin the deer and sliced the tenderloins into thin strips. Next, Woody measured two teaspoons of chili powder, one teaspoon of ground cumin and ground black pepper plus a pinch of white pepper. He commented, "I always carry fixin's," then placed the tenderloin in the mixture of spices. Next, he trimmed the fat off the deer carcass and put it in an iron skillet. After the fat was boiling, he added the seasoned tenderloins and covered the pan.

"Everyone grab a plate." Woody served each member of the party several helpings. "Our next course will be dried vegetables." Into the fat, he poured water and waited for it to come to a boil. He pulled a block of desiccated vegetables from a saddlebag and sliced chunks into the boiling broth.

Clint exclaimed, "You ain't lost your touch."

Jack and Esmeralda laughed.

Woody scowled, asking, "What's so funny?"

Jack answered, "She said that as soon as we get back to Santa Fe, she's gonna find you a wife."

"That'll be the day."

The next day the party prepared to leave. After a quick breakfast of campfire biscuits and bacon, washed down with black coffee, the party mounted and rode out of the canyon and headed west. Jack could see that Esmeralda was fine. He thought, *She's tough enough.*

Forty-Nine

Santa Fe, New Mexico – Fall 1865

The snow-capped Sangre de Cristo Mountains filled the western sky as they rode. The grassland gave way to the desert, and a cool breeze refreshed the travelers. They rode through Glorieta Pass, crested a hill, and saw Santa Fe spread before them. Esmeralda spurred her horse and set out at a run toward home. The men looked at each other. Jack commented, "Maybe we should try to keep up."

The group sped through town to the Rancho Nambe. Esmeralda jumped from her horse and ran to the door, crying, "Padre." The door sprang open. Oscar ran to his daughter and embraced her, tears running down his face. "Mi hija. Gracias a Dios."

Jack stood by his horse, and Oscar released his daughter and looked at Jack. "My daughter told me that you were going to talk to me." He smiled and stated. "That can wait. First, we eat and celebrate my daughter's return." He motioned the party to follow him into the hotel.

The party had lasted well past midnight, and the hotel guests were slow to awaken. At breakfast, Oscar approached Jack. "When you're finished, come walk with me." Jack gulped down his breakfast and headed to the door.

Oscar was waiting and motioned Jack to follow him. They crossed Independence Square. Oscar began, "Mi famila . . . " He paused. "Sorry, my family settled here a hundred years ago. My wish has always been that Esmeralda would marry a local boy and stay near her family and me, but I want her to follow her heart. I have one request." Jack followed Oscar into the San Miguel Church. They sat in a pew. Oscar clasped his hands. "Your marriage will be held in this church."

For a moment Jack was speechless. "Of course. Thank you for your blessing."

Oscar shifted and looked Jack in the eye. "Son, I could give you many reasons against marrying my daughter. But my daughter has made up her mind. The path you're taking will not be easy. Until your marriage, I ask you to follow our tradition."

Jack's smile spread across his face and he said, "Of course." He was eager to tell Esmeralda the excellent news and headed back to the hotel. His thought turned to his friend. *This spring we'll drive our cows to our land and I'll have my new wife.*

Fifty

Blanco Canyon – Early Spring 1866

After a successful hunt, the Comanche village celebrated. A feast was prepared, songs were sung, and dances were nonstop for several days. The women were busy tanning and fashioning buffalo hides into robes. Little wooden racks were constructed throughout the camp and filled with strips of buffalo meat, drying to preserve it.

The men spent their days in semi-friendly competition: wrestling, horseback races, and gambling. O'Brien, Ty, and the trappers attended the festivities. On the day set aside for horseback races, several young warriors approached Ty and in sign language invited him to enter the competition. The course was a mile long and tested skill and speed.

From the start at the edge of the village, the riders had to race up the escarpment to the top and hurtle down a different trail ending at the starting line. Ty accepted and returned to his camp to saddle his Appaloosa mare. O'Brien inquired, "Where are you going?"

"The young men invited me to join them in the horse-back race."

O'Brien's brow wrinkled. "You've accepted?"

"Sure."

"Laddie, those young bucks want to make a fool of you in front of Flower and Quanah. Watch your back."

"Don't worry, all they'll see is my horse's heels."

O'Brien saddled his horse and called to the trappers. "Boys, saddle up. We might have to make a hasty retreat."

"Why?"

"Ty's going to be in the Comanche horseback race." The men immediately sprang into action.

One trapper said to Ty, "Young fella, if we can get you back to Santa Fe alive, it'll be a miracle."

O'Brien and Ty rode to the starting line. O'Brien cautioned, "There are no rules. Watch out if you're in a bunch. Those young bucks are spending their time hatching a plan."

The starting line was not what Ty expected. Instead of a single line behind a designated spot, the riders were clustered together and smiled as they surrounded Ty. They said something that Ty could not understand and broke into laughter. While the young men enjoyed themselves, Quanah approached the group and yelled in Comanche, "Start!"

Ty, not being part of the joviality, spurred his spotted horse. His horse exploded into a run. The braves immediately took off after him. As the group approached the trail up the escarpment, riders tried to bracket Ty. As the grade steepened, Ty patted his horse and whispered, "Okay Spot, show 'em what you got." The Appaloosa was bred in the mountains of Oregon and Utah, and this was what she was born for. The spotted horse churned her rear legs while her front feet extended in front of her. Loose shale and dirt showered her pursuers. Ty held on with both hands. Several of the braves' horses faltered on the climb, forcing their riders to jump off and watch their mounts hurtle down the slope.

At the top, they had to race a quarter mile to the return trail. Several of the young warriors crested the trail and urged their mounts forward. The Indian horses were stout, and on a flat surface they were a match for the spotted horse. The course wove through cedar trees and mesquite. The Indian ponies gained on Spot. As the pursuers gained ground, the trail detoured around a stand of cedar trees. Ty whispered, "Show 'em your heels," and urged his horse at the brush. Spot hurtled over the cedars as the Indians followed the trail. Spot gained two horse lengths on their opponents. The distance narrowed as the racers approached the downhill portion of the race.

On the downhill, two of the competitors trapped Ty between them and tried to crowd his horse. The Appaloosa laid back her ears and surged into the horse on her left, knocking him off his stride, then she jigged right and cut off the other horse, forcing him to break stride. Ty and Spot slid down the embankment and hit bottom at full speed. They surged across the finish line, with Flower cheering and jumping up and down. Quanah frowned at her, and she stopped the ruckus but could not hide her broad smile.

Ty dismounted and watched the other racers cross the finish line, their faces somber.

O'Brien walked over to Ty. "Fair ride, laddie."

The celebration continued into the night. O'Brien commented, "Time to leave. Those young bucks will be working up the courage to tangle with you." Ty and the trappers followed their leader back to camp.

Fifty-One

Blanco Canyon – Spring 1866

After breakfast at the trapper's campsite, the men discussed the trade and concluded that it was time to head back to Santa Fe. The trappers knew that the Comanche would be moving to their summer range.

Quanah rode into camp and dismounted. He cradled in his arm a ceremonial hatchet/pipe and sat down by the campfire and withdrew a smoldering twig from the fire and lit the tobacco. He handed the pipe to O'Brien, who puffed and expelled a cloud of smoke and then passed it to the man next to him. The ritual continued until all had shared in the tobacco. Then he spoke, "Ty, you've proved yourself worthy. A teepee has been erected for Topsannah." He then rose and mounted his pony and rode off.

Ty queried, "What was that all about?"

The trappers and O'Brien broke out into an uproarious laugh. Finally, Ty asked, "What's so funny?"

O'Brien rubbed the tears from his eyes. "Quanah just invited you to marry Flower."

Ty scrambled to his feet.

O'Brien shouted, "Hold your horses, we've got to follow Comanche traditions!" He explained, "Someone other than you must bring the presents to the family, and if they are accepted and the girl agrees, then you can take her to her teepee, and you're married."

The trappers contributed gifts, and O'Brien unsaddled his best horse and selected another. Ty reacted. "You're not going to give away your best horse, are you?"

O'Brien smiled. "Quanah already told me how much he likes this horse." With that, he walked the two horses loaded with gifts to the village. He returned in mid-afternoon. "Laddie, tomorrow evening you will go to the village, and she'll take you to her teepee."

"What do I do then?"

"Figure it out!" The men had a hearty laugh, and Ty's face reddened.

Ty fetched a bucket of water and thought, *Time for an army bath*. Refreshed, he dressed in a newly made set of deerskin pants and shirt. He retrieved his currycomb from his saddlebag and approached Spot. "Let's get you cleaned up." The spotted horse nuzzled Ty's shoulder as the comb straightened out the horse's mane and removed built-up saddle marks.

Ty saddled up and mounted. O'Brien approached. "The boys and I are gonna hunt for a few days and prepare dried vegetables for the trip. We'll leave next week."

The trapper said, "If you need any help, I'll come running. By God, he's blushing."

Ty spurred Spot and headed for the Indian village.

As Ty exited the camp, one trapper commented, "Do black folks blush?"

O'Brien remarked, "You're about as stupid as a sack of rocks."

Flower stood in front of Quanah's teepee. She was dressed in white buckskin, with beads decorating the front of her blouse and a fringe of deer hide ruffling in the wind. Her black, auburn hair was brushed straight and glistened in the sun. She held the reins of a paint horse. Ty gazed at his new bride and thought, *She's the most beautiful woman I've ever seen.*

As Ty approached, she sprang on her horse's back and motioned Ty to follow. About a half-mile from camp, a single teepee stood with the entrance flap open. Flower tied her horse to a hitching post, grasped Ty's hand, and led him into the teepee. The floor was covered with buffalo hides. She pulled the furs covering the entrance closed.

The sun dipped below the crest of the escarpment in a burst of color. The newlyweds didn't notice.

Time flew. Ty and Flower's days were filled with walks by the stream and horseback rides exploring the canyons and grasslands surrounding Blanco Canyon. They talked about the ranch Ty and Jack hoped to start, the coming of summer, and their upcoming trip to Santa Fe.

O'Brien rode to the new couple's campsite and doffed his hat, "Well, it's time to be leaving."

Ty frowned. "The week's not up."

"It is, and we gave you an extra day."

Flower disassembled their teepee. "Ty, go get my packhorse. Quanah will help you catch him."

Fifty-Two

Ty rode to Quanah's teepee. The covering was opened. As he entered, the chief looked up and smiled. He motioned for Ty to sit. Ty began, "It's time for us to leave."

"I know."

"Topsannah asked me to come and pick up her packhorse."

Quanah smoothed his long braid. "It does my heart well to see you with my sister." Ty started to speak, but Quanah held up his hand. "The time of the people is ending. Many of the young ones want to fight to the death. This is foolish. It's time to negotiate with the white man."

Ty remarked, "I think you're wise. You'll survive as long as the blue and gray whites are at war."

"The war is over." Quanah added, "My brothers who fought with the grays have come home."

Ty stared in disbelief. "When did this happen?"

"One moon ago."

"Who won?"

"The blue soldiers."

The men sat in silence, deep in thought. Ty was the first to speak. "The United States will be unified. Now that the war is over, all eyes will turn west."

Quanah nodded. "We're going to move to another camp. I'll try to talk the young men into making peace. My sister is half-blood and will adapt to the white man's way. The black man has been freed. It will take time for the whites to accept them."

"My white father told me the same thing."

Quanah nodded. "Let's go find that packhorse."

Ty led the packhorse to their teepee. Flower had arranged the lodge poles into a travois. They tied the sled to the pack horse's Indian saddle. Flower motioned Ty to stop helping her. He protested, "I don't mind helping you."

"Watch what I do." In less than ten minutes, all their possessions were loaded and tied down.

Ty smiled and said, "I think I'll keep you around."

Flower frowned. "That's not how it works. I invited you to my teepee, and I can invite you to leave." Then a smile lit up her face as she drew him toward her.

A booming voice broke their embrace. "Enough of that, you've had your honeymoon." O'Brien and the trappers laughed. "Time for you and your lassie to mount up."

Ty took a lead rope for one mule from the trapper leading two. Flower waited with her horse and packhorse as Ty mounted Spot.

Ty thought as the group approached the escarpment, *I wonder how Jack's making out.*

Fifty-Three

Trip to Santa Fe, New Mexico – Late Spring 1866

The party rode to the top of the canyon wall. O'Brien addressed the group, "I think we should head west through the grasslands. I heard in the village that there's a lot of activity along the trails. No need to look for trouble." The trappers agreed.

Their first camp was near a playa lake, where the depression hid their campsite. As the group hobbled and unsaddled their mounts, O'Brien commented, "No teepee tonight, or fire—we'll dry camp."

The party made good progress as the miles of endless grass gave way to sandhills. Water was plentiful, and the grass deep. At the end of the first week, they stood on an overlook where the plains ended. Below them, miles of parched desert landscape shimmered in the blazing sun.

Their camp was at the foot of a gray cliff. As the group prepared to camp, O'Brien commented, "Down here you can put up your teepee. I think we'll spend a day or two here. I'll scout ahead. Tonight, we'll have a fire and eat a good meal."

Flower erected the teepee in less than a half hour. Ty sat in silence, admiring her well-rehearsed ritual. That night the group sat around discussing the next part of their journey.

One trapper commented, "Some fresh meat would taste good."

Flower responded, "While O'Brien is scouting, Ty and I will go hunting."

One trapper said, "No gunfire!"

"You watch the camp. We'll hunt."

The blazing orange sun sank into the western sky. Ty and Flower headed to the teepee. O'Brien called after them. "Laddie, have you figured it out yet?"

"By God, he's blushing again."

O'Brien threw a rock at his trapper friend.

The next morning, all agreed that the hot coffee and biscuits were a welcomed change in their diet. Flower went to her teepee and returned with a bow and a quiver of arrows. She remarked, "No gunfire."

O'Brien cast an approving eye and mounted his horse. "We'll meet back here tonight." He spurred his horse and headed west.

The trappers' readied the camp for another overnight stay. Flower pointed southwest and urged her mount. Ty followed.

Ty and Flower rode in silence. They ground-tied their mounts behind the first depression in the prairie and crept up the ridge, but saw nothing. At their third stop, a quarter of a mile away, five antelopes were grazing. They slid down the hill. Flower retrieved her bow and quiver of arrows. She motioned Ty to follow her.

They checked the wind as they disappeared into the scrub grass, upwind of their prey.

Ty mimicked her stealth movements and crawled toward the unsuspecting animals. Their journey took them the better part of an hour. About two hundred feet from the unsuspecting antelopes, Flower notched an arrow and eased into a firing position. The twang of the arrow disturbed the quiet, causing the antelopes to panic. Four of the animals sprinted away, and one laid down as if he was going to sleep.

Ty and Flower approached the prone animal. Ty thought, *She shot that arrow through its heart.*

With a smile, Flower said, "I'll start skinning and quartering the animal while you fetch the horses."

Ty's trip took about a half hour. As he dismounted, he asked, "You've gutted and quartered that animal already?"

Flower smiled and said, "Let's put the quarters over Spot's withers because you've got the better saddle to tie onto."

Ty hoisted the dead carcass and approached Spot. The horse backed up. Ty whispered, "Quiet girl, this thing can't hurt you." Ty grabbed the reins, and Spot reared. He yelled, "Calm down!"

Flower muttered, "She's never done this before. Step back. Let me have the reins."

Ty complied. Flower led the big spotted horse away from the carcass. She walked the horse in a circle and massaged its withers. Next, she led the horse to the remains of the slaughtered animal. In a quick movement, she bent down, picked up a handful of bloody entrails and smeared it on Spots nose. She walked the horse to Ty and handed him the reins. "She doesn't like the smell, but she'll get used to it."

Ty secured the quarters to his horse's saddle and smiled. "Let's get back to camp."

Fifty-Four

New Mexico Territory - Late Spring 1866

The trappers helped Ty unload the antelope. One re-marked, "That's a good catch."

While Ty and Flower had hunted, the trappers organized the camp. The mules and horses had been brushed and staked out near the cliff wall. A rock-rimmed firepit sat in the middle of the site. All the packs and saddles had been arranged in a breastwork as a protective wall.

Ty commented, "Expecting trouble?" Just as he spoke, two shots rang out.

A trapper said, "Yup. Grab your rifle and get to the barri-er. That's O'Brien warning us that he's coming in with Injuns on his tail."

Flower pointed. "There."

It took Ty a few seconds to see the rider. "He's riding to beat hell."

The trapper cautioned, "Stay down."

O'Brien's horse was lathered, eyes blazing, and running for all he was worth. Five Indians crested the hill behind O'Brien.

O'Brien's horse approached the barrier without breaking stride and hurtled over the barricade. O'Brien yelled, "Get ready for a fight." The men and Flower crouched behind their makeshift wall.

The Indians were less than a hundred feet away when the trapper yelled, "Now!" The defenders sprang to their feet.

The volley surprised the attackers. Three fell to gunshots and the fourth plunged from his horse with an arrow in his chest. All guns trained on the fifth Indian. The shots exploded into his chest, throwing him backward over his horse's rump.

The battle was over in less than a minute. All eyes turned toward O'Brien. He stepped off his horse, pointed to an arrow lodged below his left shoulder. The trapper said, "There you go again."

The trapper pulled out his knife and cut the feathered end off. "You better make yourself comfortable. It's payback time." The trapper tapped his leg. "He removed one from me up on the Snake River. Leave us be for a while. Y'all go fetch the Indian ponies and check that they're dead."

Ty and the other trapper walked to their horses and rode toward the grazing ponies. They checked each fallen Indian. The trapper commented, "She put that arrow dead center."

Flower did not follow the men. She scrambled up the escarpment and searched.

O'Brien sat propped against his saddle, and a knife lay in the fire. "Well, what are you waiting for?"

"The knife ain't hot enough. Let me take a look at that." The trapper kneeled in front of O'Brien. "Ready?" O'Brien nodded and bit down on a stick between his teeth. The trapper's hands surrounded the shaft and pushed with all his might.

O'Brien's face lost its color, he grimaced and spit out the stick, "You got 'er through?"

"Yep." The trapper circled his injured friend. "Next?" Again O'Brien nodded. A yank on the exposed arrow tip removed the shaft. The trapper retrieved the knife from the fire.

Flower approached, saying "No," and pushed the trapper aside. "This works better." In her hands, she held a prickly pear cactus leaf. She had severed it, exposing its succulent insides. "This will clean the wound."

The trapper surveyed the countryside. "We'd better skedaddle."

"No. It's late, and O'Brien needs to rest."

O'Brien tried to protest. Flower shook her head. "We'll leave at first light." Looking at the trapper, she said, "Give me a hand putting him in my teepee."

After O'Brien was made comfortable on a buffalo robe, Flower ushered the men outside. She retrieved a ceramic bowl and filled it with crushed sage. From the fire, Flower extracted a smoldering ember and dropped it on the sage. She entered the teepee and placed it near O'Brien, and a fragrant haze filled the teepee. "By tomorrow morning, you'll be able to travel." She exited the tent and closed the flap. During the night, Flower refreshed the sage and replaced the cactus bandages. O'Brien was fast asleep.

At night while Flower tended to her patient, the men broke down the camp, loaded the mules and saddled the horses. At first light, Flower touched O'Brien's arm. He asked, "How long have I been asleep?"

"All night. Time to go."

O'Brien sat up and flexed the injured shoulder. "Feels good."

After they exited the teepee, she disassembled it and secured it to her packhorse.

The trappers showed Ty how to clean up a campsite, leaving no sign they had been there.

The trappers and Ty tied the bodies of the Indians to their horses and led them to the top of the escarpment. With the plains facing them, the horses were released. The party waited until the dead riders and their horses disappeared over the horizon.

Flower cast an approving eye. "If more Apaches come, maybe this will throw them off."

Ty asked, "Can he sit his horse?"

O'Brien answered, "Laddie, I'll ride you into the ground."

The trappers exchanged glances, and one commented, "I thought we cleaned up all the horse crap."

O'Brien frowned. "Let's get started. Dry camp from here to Santa Fe."

Fifty-Five

Santa Fe, New Mexico – June 1866

It took the travelers a week to cross the rolling plains of New Mexico. Their trip rushed by. They did not have another encounter with the Apaches. Flower treated O'Brien's wound each night. He grew stronger during the journey. As they stopped on a hill overlooking Santa Fe, he remarked to Ty, "That lassie is a keeper."

Ty smiled. "I intend to. Let's get to town and find out how Jack has fared."

The party tied their horses and mules outside Rancho Nambe. The midday sun's warmth had replaced the morning chill. O'Brien suggested, "Maybe we can get a prepared meal."

As they sat, Oscar hurried to their table. "Esmeralda told me how you saved her." He looked at Ty and Flower. "She told me about your journey to win the lady's hand. It looks like you've been successful."

Ty smiled and blushed. The trapper nudged his partner.

Ty asked, "Is Jack staying here?"

"Sí, after work each night he walks with Esmeralda. They've talked to the priest about a wedding. They wanted to wait until you returned."

Esmeralda spied Flower. "Gracias a Dios." The women embraced. "You can stay with me in my room."

Ty asked, "Where's Jack?"

"He's been with Clint, working cattle."

"Is Goodnight here?"

"No. He's taken a herd of cows north. He promised to return and attend our wedding."

Ty asked, "Where can I stay?"

Flower smiled and said, "With Jack." The ladies burst into laughter and rushed from the room.

"What the hell?"

O'Brien smiled. "Get used to it, laddie. Women are strange creatures."

Jack led Ty to their room. Ty slumped on his bed. "What do you make of that? Flower and I were married in Quanah's village. The wedding consisted of her people building her a teepee, and she invited me in. Now she's moved in with her girlfriend, and I'm stuck with you."

Jack spoke, "These people have strange customs. Before I talked to Esmeralda's dad, we'd take walks and sit by ourselves. Now anytime I'm with her, we are followed around by a bunch of women." Jack scratched his head. "I asked one of the Spanish fellas what was going on." He said, "It's our custom."

"Maybe it's time to set a wedding date?"

"Agreed." They both laughed.

Fifty-Six

Santa Fe, New Mexico – June 1866

Jack reached into his saddlebag, which hung from the bedpost. "While you were gone, you got a letter." He handed it to Ty.

Ty opened the letter and read it to himself. Then he paraphrased. "This is from my father. He says now that the war is over, the Union army is running everything. They've accused him of being a slave owner. He's not sure if he'll be able to keep his plantation together."

"It's his property. How can anyone take it?"

"I don't know."

"In my letter to him, I explained our partnership and the land purchase. He's transferred a substantial amount of money to a bank in Houston and has written the bank president with instructions to hold the money and to disburse it at my discretion."

"My words ain't as fancy as yours, but I get the gist of it. My dad sent me my share of the profits in gold coins."

They discussed how they'd pay Goodnight for the land. That settled, Jack added, "We have enough money to purchase the land and buy the equipment we'll need."

Ty scratched his head. "We've laid out enough work to last us the next ten years. We're gonna need help."

"Yep, we've got a lot of planning to do."

Included in the partners' plans was Jack's marriage to Esmeralda.

The wedding day was set for June 13th. The service was conducted by the pastor of the San Miguel Mission at 3 p.m.

After the ceremony, the newly married couple walked to the Rancho Nambe. The celebration lasted until midnight. Local musicians played mariachi music. Mountains of food were prepared by Esmeralda's family.

The bride and groom stood at the entrance and greeted their guests. Each person was introduced. "This is my aunt. This is my cousin. This is my second cousin . . . "

Finally, Jack whispered to Esmeralda, "How many relatives do you have?"

"More coming, this is only the local relatives. The people from the ranches will be here later."

"Oh, boy."

Ty walked over, "How long is this going to last?"

"'Til she runs out of relatives."

They turned as five more relatives burst through the door and surrounded the bride and groom.

Ty had accompanied the wedding party, which included Flower. As they returned from the service, Ty stated, "You can't stay with your girlfriend tonight."

"I know, my teepee is set up outside of town."

"Am I invited?"

Her face lit up. "If you promise to be good."

.

Fifty-Seven

Santa Fe, New Mexico – June 1866

On Monday, June 15th, Ty, Jack, and Goodnight met at the newly opened bank.

The banker, an easterner recently arrived from New York, greeted them. "Good morning gentlemen, my name is Gerald Griswold. How can I be of assistance?" The rotund, balding banker extended his soft, sweaty hand.

"The name's Goodnight. This here is Ty Jones and Jack Donaldson."

Ty continued, "Jack and I have been told that certain funds have been deposited with your bank for us by our fathers."

"I see, but first, I have to see your credentials." He walked to his desk and sat.

The partners handed the banker several papers. With a start, Griswold exclaimed, "Jack, you served with the Union, and Ty fought for the Confederacy."

Goodnight frowned. "The war's over. Are you satisfied with their credentials?"

"Yes, yes, certainly."

Goodnight continued. "This transaction is between the JA Ranch and Ty and Jack's Flat Top Mountain Ranch."

The banker's face lost color. "Are you Charles Goodnight?"

"Last time I looked."

The banker burst out of his chair. "Please have a seat at the conference table. I'll have coffee and refreshments brought."

"That ain't needed. We need to have the funds transferred from their account to mine."

"Certainly."

It took several minutes to conclude the transfers. As the men exited the bank, Griswold announced to the staff. "That was Charles Goodnight!" The local employees smirked.

Goodnight suggested, "Let's stop at the cantina for a drink to toast your new ranch." The men sat at a table.

The former Confederate soldier was tending bar. "What's your pleasure, men?"

The orders placed, the bartender hurried to the bar and returned with the drinks. Goodnight stated, "We'll only take the drinks if you let us pay."

The bartender responded, "Fair enough. Everyone knows the South lost the war." He looked at Ty. "It's about time.

Nothing good comes out of a war. What's next for you, fellas?"

Ty answered, looking at Jack, "My partner and I have purchased land from Mr. Goodnight. We plan to start a ranch."

The bartender's eyes glistened as he said, "You married Oscar's daughter, a fine girl. I've known her since she was a baby. A new ranch and a new wife, I reckon you've done right nice. Have another drink with me." The men laughed as the bartender returned with another round and one for himself. "Here's to you, boys. Good luck!"

Fifty-Eight

———◆•◆•◆———

Santa Fe, New Mexico – Summer 1866

The next morning, Ty and Flower joined Jack and Esmeralda for breakfast. Jack commented to Ty, "When we finish eating, we have to plan our trip to the ranch. Maybe the girls can keep themselves busy."

Esmeralda looked at Flower, then spoke. "Flower and I will help you."

Jack frowned and said, "I guess this is what men complain about after they get married."

Ty remarked, "Okay, let's figure out what food we should take."

Jack suggested, "Some salt pork, canned beans, and coffee."

"That'll do it."

Esmeralda frowned. "You men arrange for a wagon and a team of mules. Go check on our cattle. We'll handle the food."

The men nodded and looked at their wives. Flower remarked, "Don't you two have work to do?"

Ty and Jack headed for their horses.

Ty asked, "Where are the cattle grazing?"

"At Goodnight's place, five miles south of town."

As they rode, Jack filled Ty in on their herd. "Our cows are mixed in with Goodnight's. We didn't brand the cows we bought, but the others are branded. We'll have to separate the cows. There's a corral with a working chute on his place. We have permission to use it. Clint and the cowboys will help us. We'll have to pay them for the day's work."

Ty answered, "That's fair. We've got to come up with a brand for the cattle."

Jack stated, "How about JD under an outline of the Flat Top Mountain? We can have a blacksmith make up our branding iron."

Fifty-Nine

Santa Fe, New Mexico – Summer 1866

Jack remarked, "Our cows have had some calves. It won't be a problem if we separate them from their mamas for half a day. They'll pair up once their mamas are set free."

They arrived at Goodnight's place and met Clint. "While you two were off getting yourselves married, we've been riding night herd. I figure we'll be splitting the duty starting tonight."

They rode through the cows with Clint and discussed plans for the branding and sorting of the cattle. Jack was impressed by the condition of the animals, and that about half of the cows had calves. Jack asked, "Do you think the new calves will be a problem?"

Clint answered, "No, the babies will stay next to their mothers. If there are any calves born during the trip, we'll have to let the newborn suckle his first milk before we move on." He scratched his head and said, "It'll probably take a week or two before you're ready to move. I'd bet most of the calves will be on the ground before you leave."

It was approaching midday. "We've got to get back to town and grab some food and our bedrolls. We'll be back before too long."

The men spurred their horses and trotted to the Rancho Nambe. Their wives were busy canning vegetables.

"Well, it looks like we've got to watch over the cattle tonight."

Esmeralda asked, "Do you need something to eat?"

"Yep."

"Go get the stuff you need to camp out and we'll make you a sack of food."

Ty and Jack took about fifteen minutes to gather their bedrolls and a change of clothes. They loaded a packhorse and returned to the Rancho. "We're packed."

Flower handed Ty a bulging burlap sack. "This should hold both of you for a couple of days."

"We're only going to stay the night."

"Don't worry, I'll stay with Esmeralda."

Ty looked at Jack. "Is this more of that married stuff?"

"I reckon."

After Ty and Jack had established their camp for the night, Clint rode up. "We'd better get started sorting and branding tomorrow. Goodnight's anxious to get moving. He plans to drive the herd to the Palo Duro, then we'll separate them and help you drive your cows to your place."

Jack and Ty mounted their horses. Ty commented, "Before we start, we need a branding iron."

"Draw out your brand and give it to me. I'll have the blacksmith make it tomorrow. As soon as it's ready, I'll be back, and we'll get started. In the morning, separate out your cows." Clint spurred his horse and headed for town.

The partners split the night watch. At first light, Jack made fresh coffee. Ty stepped off his horse. "The cattle are settled. Let's see what we've got for breakfast."

Jack opened the burlap bag. "Look here, this is loaded with stuffed tortillas." The coffee grounds settled on the bottom of the pot, and it was ready.

The men sat and ate their meal. Ty commented, "That was good."

"Some of this married stuff ain't so bad."

The partners chuckled as they mounted their horses. They had cattle to gather.

Clint arrived around midday. "Look at that, the greenhorns have the cows corralled and sorted. You boys will make a hand, someday." The cowboys with Clint laughed.

Jack smiled and said, "If you stop laughing, we'll have lunch and get to work." Tortillas were passed around. Fresh coffee filled their cups.

A cowboy noted, "Whoever made these vittles has earned their spurs."

The branding took the balance of the day. Duties were rotated. One man roped and dragged each cow, and two others wrestled the cow to the ground and held it while the brand was applied. The cow was turned loose after she found her calf, and the cowboys herded them out of the gate. It was nearly dark when the task was complete.

Clint relaxed near the fire. "If you have any more grub, we'll watch the cows tonight."

Jack handed the burlap bag to Clint and nodded at Ty. They mounted their horses. Out of earshot, Ty said, "Time for some more of that married stuff."

Sixty

Santa Fe, New Mexico — Summer 1866

The newlywed couples met for a late breakfast. Jack whispered to Ty, "It sure felt good to sleep indoors again."

Ty smiled. "That's for sure."

As the couples sat, Esmeralda asked, "When do you think we're going to our new ranch?"

Ty replied, "Probably next week. We're finished branding our cows."

The women almost asked in unison, "What does our brand look like?" They laughed at their shared thought.

Jack described it. The women nodded. Flower noted, "Both families living under the Flat Top Mountain." Smiles all around as the preparations for the trip were discussed.

Ty said to them, "Tonight, we have to ride night herd."

Flower said, "I'll keep your spot warm."

The day was spent inventorying the equipment they had to purchase.

Jack noted, "We'll need a wagon and a team of mules."

Esmeralda's lips curled at the corners. "We've already purchased the wagon, and Papa let us have two of his best mules."

The women led their men to the back of the Nambe. There, two hobbled mules grazed near a prairie schooner. Jack smiled. "Well, I'll be."

Flower said, "Tonight we'll start packing for the trip."

The women walked with their men to the stable. With their horses saddled, the men led their horses toward the Nambe, and their wives accompanied them.

At the hotel, Esmeralda motioned the men to wait. "We've packed some food." The women disappeared inside and returned with a burlap sack.

Smiles lit up their faces as the two partners spurred their horses.

Ty noted, "This married stuff ain't so bad."

Clint greeted the partners. "Howdy boys. I see you've got another sack. We haven't finished the first one. Those gals of yours sure know how to cook."

Jack asked, "When do you think we'll be ready to leave?"

"I think by the day after tomorrow. I'll get some other boys to ride night herd while we pack for the trip."

Ty stated, "I appreciate that we've got a lot of gear to pack."

Jack looked at Ty and added, "We've been talking, and we'd like to hire two hands to help us get the ranch set up and help with the cows."

Clint removed his sombrero and scratched his head. "How about old Woody and me? We've done enough wandering."

Jack asked, "You won't mind working for a couple of greenhorns?"

"Nope. So long as your women do the cooking."

Sixty-One

Raton Pass – Fall 1866

The partners met the next morning to discuss their plans. Goodnight joined them.

"Howdy. I see you ladies are still putting up with these two."

Flower answered, "Haa."

Goodnight responded in Comanche, "Yes, a good sign—is he still allowed in your teepee?"

Ty surprised Goodnight by answering in Comanche, "Haa."

Goodnight's face lit up. Looking at Esmeralda and speaking in Spanish, he said "I hear you married the gringo?"

Jack responded in kind. "Sí."

"Well, I guess I can't have private conversations with your ladies." His lips curled into a smile. "Are you ready to head out to your new ranch?"

The couples nodded in agreement. Jack added, "We've hired Clint and Woody to work with us on the ranch."

"I know, they told me. Good men like them will always be welcomed in my outfit. They'll be a big help. You fellas have come a long way, but there's a passel of things y'all need to learn."

Ty answered, "We know that. When do you want to set out?"

"We'd better move out day after tomorrow. I have information that a large group of Yankee soldiers is headed this way. We need to make sure the blue bellies know who owns the land. I've been visiting with the Texas governor and the land commissioner in Austin, and our titles are filed. The army is running roughshod over the South. We have the law on our side."

Ty shook his head. "My dad wrote to me about what the Army is doing in Louisiana. We should get moving." All agreed.

The ladies sprang to their feet. "We have much to do."

Goodnight added, "We have to see to our cattle."

The day of departure drew near. Ty and Jack spent their days gathering Goodnight's and their cattle into one herd. They planned to detour around Santa Fe and head for Raton Pass. The night before departure, the travelers gathered at Rancho Nambe. Oscar and his wife laid out a sumptuous meal. Mrs. Morales made Jack promise to visit often.

Esmeralda was cheerful and vowed to return home when possible.

The morning came early. The only hint of the coming daylight was a gray shading in the eastern sky. Mr. and Mrs. Morales and their staff rose early to prepare a light breakfast. Flower and Esmeralda were dressed in buckskin trail clothes.

Mrs. Morales commented, "Dio, my baby looks like a cowboy." She embraced Flower, saying, "You've been like a daughter. I'm happy that you'll be with my hija." The group mounted and rode out.

Tears streamed down Esmeralda's face. Jack reached over and squeezed her hand. Mr. Morales lifted his hand, turned, and put his arm around his wife and led her into the Rancho. "Don't worry Mama, Jack's a good man and will take care of our little girl."

The crew gathered the herd two miles north of town. The Sangre de Cristo Mountains loomed in the distance. The wagons and cows were formed at the rear, and extra mounts grazed under the watchful eye of the cowboys. The herd, numbering one thousand, stood in silence, surrounded by cowboys and vaqueros. The partners and their wives joined the herders. Goodnight rode to the head of the cattle. "Let's get moving."

The riders surrounding the cattle waited as the men riding drag whistled and slapped their chaps. Slowly the herd followed Goodnight as he moved off.

Esmeralda rode her horse and watched the cattle. No one but Flower noticed her brush away a tear.

That day they covered fifteen miles. That night the cattle settled in a grass-filled valley next to a flowing stream. Clint assigned the night shifts. Woody set up for the evening meal. Flower and Esmeralda made the fire and laid out the cookware. Woody commented, "That ain't your job." The ladies smiled and continued working. "That's why I never married—women don't listen."

They prepared the meal and the cowboys lined up. Slim commented, "This sure looks good. I guess the women are teaching Woody how to cook." Woody threw a hot biscuit at Slim's head.

"Next time, it'll be a rock." Everyone laughed.

On the morning the herd was scheduled to enter Raton Pass, Goodnight addressed the group. "It looks clear, going through the pass. We'll rest the cows and horses when we get through. Once we're clear of the pass, I'll ride ahead and scout out our campsites."

The trip through Raton Pass was peaceful. The pine forest and cooler temperatures were a relief from the summer heat at the lower altitudes. As the herd moved out of the pass, they camped near a stream. The next morning, Goodnight and two cowboys rode out.

Clint assigned shifts. The party would be camped for several days. Flower erected her teepee. She motioned to Esmeralda. "We'll sleep inside tonight." Ty and Jack exchanged shocked glances. "There's enough room for all of us." Smiles replaced the partners' horrified expressions. Esmeralda and Flower doubled over with laughter.

Sixty-Two

Texas High Plains – Fall 1866

Goodnight returned to camp on the fourth morning as breakfast was being served. "We've scouted the next week's camps, and it looks like it'll be alright, but the first day is going to be a long one. It's twenty miles to the next water."

Clint remarked, "The cows are rested and full. If we get an early start, we should be able to make it. Y'all be ready to move at first light."

As promised, the day was a long one. Several newborn calves had to be loaded onto the wagons for the trip. Clint told the crew, "Keep an eye on the young'uns, if you see one get too far behind, rope it and put it in the wagon."

By the time the herd reached the campsite, another five calves were riding in the wagon. When the cows settled, the calves in the cart were turned loose. The mama cows mooed, calling their babies to them. Clint's face lit up. "Good job, men. Ain't nothing better than seeing calves with their mamas." The cowboys agreed.

Goodnight returned from another scouting trip. "We're two days from Palo Duro. Today, I saw a troop of blue belly cavalry parading across the plains. We'll probably bump into them."

The next two days were uneventful. The night before arriving at Goodnight's ranch, a party of troopers entered the camp. At the head of the company of soldiers sat a Union officer. He reined his horse by the campfire and stepped down. Speaking to no one, he said, "Good evening. Lieutenant Johnson, at your service."

Ty's face lit up, and he exclaimed, "Major Johnson!"

Johnson turned to face Ty. "I'll be, its Sergeant Jones. I didn't think I'd run into you out here." The mounted troopers shifted in their saddles and exchanged glances. He turned to his first sergeant and said, "Find a place to set up camp. I'll be along presently."

"Yes, sir." The sergeant motioned to his troopers, "Let's move."

Goodnight approached the former Confederate soldiers. "The name's Charles Goodnight. Did you serve with Ty?"

"Yes, sir."

"He called you major? You fought for the Confederacy?"

"Yes, sir. We fought at Vicksburg together."

He pointed to his epaulet. "This was the only billet available with Colonel Mackenzie."

Goodnight scratched his head. "I don't understand."

"The war's over, and soldiering is all I know. I was at West Point when the war started. I resigned my Union commission and went home to fight for the Confederacy."

"Sit down and have some coffee. Tell us how things have shaken out."

The group gathered around Johnson and peppered him with questions. Johnson tried to answer all the questions. He recounted how the Union Army was occupying the southern states. Ty asked about Mr. Boudreaux.

"Ty, your dad told me you headed west. He's been able to keep the carpetbaggers off your land."

Ty asked, "Carpetbaggers?"

"That's a group of northern vultures who invaded the South, buying land at ten cents on the dollar." He smiled. "I've got to hand it to the old gentleman, those Yankees are no match for your dad."

Ty answered, "That's good to hear."

"I'd better get back to my troops. I have to scout another fifty miles and report back to Colonel Mackenzie."

Goodnight asked, "What are you looking for?"

"Comanches." Johnson mounted his horse and followed after his troopers.

After the lieutenant was out of camp, Goodnight remarked, "They ain't gonna find them heading that way."

Flower addressed the group. "My people call their colonel 'Bad Hand.'"

Ty asked, "Why?"

Flower held up her hand and made a cutting motion at her fingers.

The group finished their meal and broke out their sleeping bags.

Sixty-Three

Pala Duro Canyon – Fall 1866

Clint raised his hand and stated, "We're here." The Goodnight headquarters were located one mile east of the canyon and ten miles below the start of the canyon. He'd constructed pens for his horses and a dugout for living quarters. The mesquite-populated plain gave way to the canyon. A switchback trail wove down the escarpment to a branch of the Red River.

The cows settled down on the prairie. Goodnight addressed the group. "Let's take it easy for a couple of days. Then we'll sort out Ty and Jack's cows and help herd them to the Flat Top Mountain."

The partners and their wives selected an area to erect Flower's teepee. The men gathered wood as their wives prepared the evening meal. The fire simmered in the heat of the plains. In the distance, a dust devil skipped across the plains. Flower noted, "The land is saying hello."

Jack smiled. "In a couple of days, we'll be setting up on our own land."

Esmeralda pointed toward heaven. "We don't own the land, we're only occupying it for a short time."

Clint and Woody joined the couples. "Howdy folks. Looks like we're in time for dinner."

The women handed the men plates they had prepared for them. Woody smiled and said, "Thank you, ma'am."

Ty asked, "How long will it take to get to our place?"

Clint rubbed his beard. "Three days." He chewed on his food and added, "Then the work starts."

In the evening, the couples and the new employees discussed the upcoming trip. As dusk crept up the wall of the canyon, Woody stated, "It's time to start night herd." As he finished, the howl of a coyote broke the silence and was answered by two others.

Clint nodded at Woody. "We'll ride the first watch." Looking at Ty and Jack, he asked, "Is that okay?"

Esmeralda spoke, "Jack and I will relieve you at ten tonight."

Flower added, looking at Ty, "We'll take over at two in the morning. That will allow everyone to get a decent night's sleep. During the day, we only need one herd rider. We'll set the schedule at breakfast tomorrow."

The four men looked aghast. Clint broke the silence. "Woody, let's get started."

The two night riders saddled their horses and rode toward the herd. Woody spoke, "Now you know why I never married."

"Yup."

The next morning after breakfast, the group assembled. One of Goodnight's cowboys was watching the cattle. Clint spoke, "The coyotes were circling the cows, but we ran them off. The coyotes are too smart."

Flower pointed to a pole stuck in the ground with two dead coyotes hanging from it.

"I didn't hear no shooting."

Flower patted her bow.

"Well, I'll be!"

Woody shook his head and said, "Don't say it."

The men all enjoyed a good laugh and a new respect for the ladies.

The watches were established and the day planned. Clint asked, "Do y'all think Woody and I should scout the trail to our ranch?"

All agreed. Flower volunteered, "I can make you a new set of moccasins from the coyote fur. I have some cured buffalo hide for the soles. When winter comes, you'll appreciate warm feet."

Woody smiled. "Yes, ma'am. Clint, let's get moving." They mounted their horses.

Esmeralda handed Woody a small burlap sack containing food for the trip.

Sixty-Four

The Flat Top Mountain Ranch – Fall 1866

The cattle were rested, and the calves stayed by their mamas' sides. There were no further incidents with coyotes. Clint and Woody had scouted their route to their new home. Clint woke up, and the sun was a sliver in the western sky. "Time to get started." He took his place in front of the herd. Woody's job was to ride the supply wagon. The young wives led the gear-laden mules. Ty and Jack rode drag, and Goodnight's cowboys flanked the herd.

Slapping on buckskinned legs and soft whistles encouraged the cows to follow Clint. At midday, the cows stood knee-high in prairie grass along a branch of the Red River.

Woody handed out refried bean-stuffed tortillas. One cowboy remarked, "These are mighty good."

"Don't thank me." He motioned to the young wives. "The ladies made 'em."

Clint called a halt at midday. "This is a good place to stop. We made good time today, no sense pushing the calves. We have another two men to ride night herd."

Esmeralda and Flower gathered firewood as Woody prepared the dried vegetables and deer meat. The aroma of coffee filled the air. Esmeralda said, "You've got to let me know your secret, this deer meat is delicious."

"Yup."

Esmeralda sat expectantly.

Woody answered, "Someday."

The party crossed Los Lingus creek midday on their third day. The area was grass covered and flat. Clint stated, "This is good pasture. We can turn the mules loose with the cows. Mules just naturally hate coyotes, so they'll help protect the herd."

Jack stated, "When we camped here last time, I thought this would be a good place to locate our headquarters. We'll get camp set up before dark." He surveyed the group, and no one objected.

At the campsite, Flower quickly assembled the teepee. The party settled down. Ty commented, "Across the stream, there's a blind canyon. The cliffs rise up twenty feet on three sides. We should be able to make a corral for the horses tomorrow."

Jack asked, "Clint, what do you think?"

"A good spot. We'll cut cedar posts tomorrow and run a couple of strands of barbed wire and build a gate. Shouldn't take no time at all."

Ty asked, "Shouldn't we work on housing for you and Woody?"

"The livestock comes first. We can camp out. If it rains, we'll get into the wagon. You fellas and your wives can live in the teepee for a while. We'd better get started—Goodnight's men will want to be getting back."

The next week was spent completing the stockade for the horses. Not far from the corral, an outcropping of rock provided the back wall to a combination dugout and cabin for Woody and Clint.

Cedar posts formed the front door and ceiling. The men had cleared the brush and tamped down the earthen floor. Esmeralda and Flower approached, carrying a stack of buffalo hides. Flower smiled and held them out. "For your new home."

Woody and Clint exchanged glances. Jack looked at Ty, saying, "Look, they're blushing."

The summer days passed quickly. Woody remark to Jack, "Y'all are pretty handy with an ax and saw."

"My dad taught me well."

One person watched the cows around the clock, and the duty shifted every four hours. The work on the corral proceeded rapidly. The women trimmed the branches off the posts, each standing eight feet. Two men dug the postholes. To close the canyon took one hundred posts. Each posthole was three feet deep. They trimmed thin poplar trees to form a top rail, and carved a notch on each post to fit the topping. From the ground up, they ran five strands of barbed wire, held in place by iron staples. Jack spent two days making the gate, framed in birch and cedar posts. Looking at the finished product, he announced. "That'll do it."

Ty stated, "Let's get the horses put up and celebrate."

As winter approached, Clint said, "We've got to herd the cattle into the streambed. There's lots of grass, and the dripping aquifer should run water all winter. We'll have to make sure pools of water don't ice over."

Woody said, "This would be a good time to see if we can't shoot a buffalo."

Flower remarked. "Do that, and I'll prepare the meat for storage and make a new winter coat."

Jack conferred with Ty, then announced, "Why don't you and Clint go buffalo hunting after we move the cattle?"

Broad smiles filled Clint's and Woody's face. "We'll bring back the biggest bull we can."

Sixty-Five

The Flat Top Mountain Ranch – Winter 1866

The valley that ended at the Flat Top Mountain had been the winter home for buffalo since the end of the ice age. Protected from the fury of winter storms that turned the plains into a frozen tundra, the animals gathered by the streams and sheltering trees.

A ten-mile view rewarded those who climbed the Flat Top Mountain. Clint and Woody hobbled their pack mules at the beginning of the deer trail to the summit. They gave their horses their heads and relaxed as their mounts picked their way up the path. Once they reached the top, the men dismounted and used a pair of army binoculars and took turns surveying the plains.

"Over there," Clint whispered, pointing, and handed the binoculars to Woody. The dark brown animals stood out against the newly fallen snow.

Woody commented, "Remember when this valley was thick with buffs?"

"Yup. No more. There are three old bulls with that group. We'll get close and camp for the night. We'll have better luck at first light."

The men camped in a copse of oak trees and hobbled their mules and horses. Woody remarked, "Let's dry camp tonight. The girls packed enough food to last three days."

"I'm getting to like those girls."

"The boys have good wives. I think Esmeralda wants us to go with her to visit her father in the spring. She's mentioned something about her old maid cousin."

"You go. I can't leave in the spring—the cows will start calving."

"Both of us will have to stay." The men laughed and spread out their bedrolls.

At first light, Woody and Clint tied their horses to trees, shouldered their high-powered rifles, and crept up on the herd of buffalo as they lay resting. With hand signals, they agreed on their target. Clint aimed below the bull's shoulder and pulled the trigger. The shot was muffled by the falling snow. The remaining buffaloes scattered.

"Nice shot. I hate chasing wounded animals."

The pair retrieved their horses and pack mules. When they reached the fallen animal, two wolves were circling it. Two quick shots and two wolves ended their hunt. "Looks like we'll have fresh hides for coats and gloves."

"Yup. Let's get to work."

Sixty-Six

The Flat Top Mountain Ranch – December 1866

The next day, with the hides packed and the buffalo meat stashed in saddlebags, they rode back to their new home. Flower and Esmeralda admired the skins and unpacked.

The group decided that tonight they would prepare a feast of fresh buffalo meat and vegetables. Flower gathered wild onions and edible roots, and plucked ears from a prickly pear cactus. She hung the stomach of the butchered buffalo from four stout sticks. She placed a mixture of vegetables in the stomach pouch, filled it with water, retrieved hot rocks from the fire, and placed them in the bag.

Woody stated, "I've watched this prepared." He asked. "Is it alright if I add some of my spices to the vegetables?"

Flower smiled and nodded her head.

Woody dashed to the dugout and returned with a selection of herbs. He and Flower sniffed each plant. They agreed on the addition and sat admiring their handiwork.

Jack and Ty returned from checking the cows.

Jack sniffed the air. "Smells good. When do we eat?"

The group sat around after dinner. The conversation turned to the next year. Clint remarked, "Those yearling steers need to be sold before summer. The mamas are heavy with new calves."

Jack asked, looking at Clint and Woody, "Do y'all think Esmeralda and I could ride to Santa Fe and visit her family?"

Esmeralda spoke up, "I thought Clint and Woody could come with us."

The two older men shook their heads, and Woody added, "The cows know where the water is, and there's plenty of grass, but we'll have to check them each day. We can't leave with new calves coming. You young folks enjoy yourselves."

"Ty and Flower will be in camp. One of you should come with us and make sure we don't get lost."

The two cowboys scowled. Clint spoke, "Short straw." He picked up two twigs and broke them into uneven lengths, and put the sticks behind his back. The pieces looked even as he held his hand out for Woody to choose.

Woody studied the sticks, decided, and picked one. He held it up next to Clint's. "Dang, I got the short straw."

Clint chuckled, "Say hello to the cousin."

The couples shrugged, and Ty commented, "What are you talking about?"

Clint blurted out, "Nothing."

Woody threw his stick at his partner.

The next two days were spent preparing for Jack and Esmeralda's trip to Santa Fe.

Ty wrote a letter to his father. He mentioned that Major (now Lieutenant) Johnson had visited him. He described the ranch and their plans for the future.

The trio would travel light, taking only necessary clothes and easy-to-prepare meals.

The group discussed the projects to be undertaken in the spring. They would buy mules in Santa Fe to transport their supplies.

Esmeralda looked at Flower. "We'd like permanent housing."

Jack commented, "I was thinking the same thing."

Ty nodded agreement and added, "We'll have to build a bunkhouse for Woody and Clint, too."

The travelers left for Santa Fe at first light on December 1st. As they rode off, Clint asked Woody, "Should I make another dugout?"

"No!"

The traveler's horses climbed the escarpment. Light snow covered the ground, and the cedar trees glistened in the morning sun. Esmeralda sighed, "I'll miss our piece of heaven, but I'm looking forward to seeing Mama and Papa."

Jack smiled. "We'll be back."

Sixty-Seven

Santa Fe, New Mexico – December 1866

The travelers arrived in Santa Fe on December 10th. They entered the Rancho Nambe. Seated at a table was Sean O'Brien. He looked up at Jack and said, "I see you've still got your hair."

Mr. Morales ran from behind his desk. "Mama, Esmeralda está aquí." Mrs. Morales burst out of the kitchen and surrounded her daughter and husband with her arms, tears streaming down her face.

"Mama, no llores." She brushed away her mother's tears.

"I'll start preparing a special meal." Mrs. Morales headed for the kitchen.

Esmeralda smiled. "I'm going to help Mama."

Mr. Morales said, "Have a seat. I'll get you a cup of coffee."

The three men sat at a round oak table with matching chairs. Jack said, "It's been a long time since I've sat in a chair." Morales and O'Brien laughed.

O'Brien inquired, "How's ranching?"

"It's going good. We had to force Woody to come with us."

"Aye, those old cowboys would rather be with cattle than people."

Morales stated, "My daughter looks happy."

"She's a wonderful wife. She keeps talking about babies."

"Just like her mama."

O'Brien nodded. "It's a woman's thing."

Jack continued, "It's been quiet. We had a visit by a troop of cavalry." He described the meeting.

O'Brien noted, "Now that the war is over, a lot of former Rebel soldiers are joining the Union army. There's going to be a major push to get the Indians on reservations. When we visited Quanah's camp, he told me he knew it was inevitable, but he would hold out as long as he can. Did Ty's friend say who his commanding officer is?"

"Colonel Mackenzie."

"I've heard about him. He's persistent and smart. I hope old Quanah and his people make peace." O'Brien shook his head. "I heard that Goodnight sold most of his cattle while the prices were high and is going to stay out of Palo Duro until things settle down."

"This spring, we're gonna sell our yearlings and older cows. We haven't seen hide nor hair of Indians."

"Laddie, that's because of your partner's wife. They know you're there."

"How was your winter trapping?" Jack asked O'Brien.

"We did well, but I've decided to quit trapping. The northern tribes are getting organized to drive the white man from their lands. One of the medicine men has them believing that if they do a ghost dance, they'll be bulletproof." O'Brien's usual bright eyes darkened, "A band of Crows jumped us at the Tetons. We beat them off and thought we were finished with them. We moved our camp, and the Injuns followed. We fought a running battle 'til we got to Raton Pass. The Injuns killed Tiny and Big Foot, but they didn't get their hair. I'm quitting trapping until things settle down."

"Are you going to be transporting supplies across the Santa Fe Trail?"

"Aye, come spring."

They discussed the list of supplies and materials they needed to purchase. Mr. Morales commented, "We'll be able to visit our grandchildren."

"You sure can, Papa."

O'Brien scowled.

Jack looked at the trapper. "And you too."

The men enjoyed a round of laughter.

The next day, Jack visited the banker. Mr. Griswold bounded out of his office. "Nice to see you, Mr. Donaldson. How's your ranch?"

Jack answered, "It's coming together. Our cows are doing great, and we'll probably take a hundred head to the market in the summer."

"Your timing is right. Have you thought about selling cattle to the army?"

"No."

"Well, you should. The western states are going to be flooded with soldiers. I hear they also need horses."

Jack nodded. "Something to think about."

Griswold continued, "I received a delivery of mail for you and Mr. Jones." He removed four letters tied in a ribbon and handed them to Jack.

"Thank you. I've contracted with Sean O'Brien to deliver two wagons of supplies. Our arrangement is one-half now and the balance when the delivery is complete. I've told O'Brien that you'll handle the payments. Is that okay?"

"That's what we're here for. I'll prepare a draft for your signature. Either of you can sign for the partnership. We'll also need a final payment authorization that approves disbursement to Mr. O'Brien once the goods are received."

"That's good. I'll stop by, day after tomorrow?"

"We'll have everything prepared." Mr. Griswold stood and extended his sweaty hand.

That night at dinner, Jack explained to Woody and Esmeralda what he'd set up for their supplies. "The banker said the army will be looking for horses. What do you think of buying horses, breaking them, and selling them to the army?"

Woody rubbed his neck. "Not a bad idea, but we seem to be busy every day."

"I thought we could pick up maybe fifty horses and hire two cowboys. They could work with the horses. Once our supplies come in, we could build fences. The new men can also help build new houses."

Woody stated, "I'll scout around for horses."

Esmeralda perked up. "That sounds wonderful. I was thinking of inviting my cousin to dinner tomorrow."

Woody stood. "Ma'am, I'll be heading out to find the horses. I'd better go and get ready." With that, he stood and bolted for the door.

Esmeralda quizzed, "Did I say something wrong?"

Sixty-Eight

Santa Fe, New Mexico – Early 1867

January started cold and dry. The travelers prepared to return to the ranch.

Woody sat with Al and Bo, the new cowboys, and Jack. "I think we should avoid Raton Pass and take the south route."

Al asked, "Is there enough water along the way for the horses?"

"It'll be tough, but if we can make good time, we'll be okay."

All was ready. Mr. and Mrs. Morales walked with Jack and Esmeralda to their horses. Mrs. Morales asked, "Where are the cowboys?"

Jack answered, "They've already started with the pack animals and the horses. We'll catch up with them."

Mrs. Morales' eyes misted over as she said, "Vaya con Dios."

The newlyweds spurred their horses. By midday, they caught up with Woody and the cowboys. That night at dinner, Woody talked to the group. "You men seem able to handle the horses." He looked at Jack, "Do y'all think you can tend to the pack animals?"

"Yup."

"I'm gonna scout ahead. I'll leave early."

The next evening, Woody rode into camp. "We've got trouble. Injuns ain't far behind me. You boys got the stock hobbled?"

"Yes, sir."

"Make sure your best horse is saddled and ground-tied near us. We've got to build a breastwork."

Everyone sprang into action. The travelers dug pits behind the stacked saddlebags. Everyone had a rifle.

Woody addressed the group. "It looks like a full moon. Them Injuns might make a run at the horses before dawn. I'm gonna sneak out to the edge of the herd and pick off any rustlers."

Jack spoke up. "Not alone." He stood.

Woody held up his hand. "No. You stay with your wife. Al, you come with me."

The night grew lighter as the moon rose, but only the coyotes celebrated its coming.

The three at the campsite took turns sleeping. The moon was at its fullest when the crack of a rifle broke the silence. Another rifle shot rang out, then a third and a fourth.

Jack noted, "They're moving around. They want the Indians to think they've run into a large force."

As the sun broke the eastern horizon, Woody and Al walked back to camp. Four scalps hung from Woody's belt. Esmeralda averted her eyes. Woody commented, "When the other braves find their bodies, they'll think twice about attacking us. Let's get moving."

The group broke camp and moved out at a fast trot. Jack joined the two cowboys. Esmeralda and Woody led the pack animals.

They didn't know what awaited them.

Sixty-Nine

The Flat Top Mountain Ranch – Early Spring 1867

Ty, Flower, and Clint had been busy since the departure of Jack, Esmeralda, and Woody. Their practice was to share their evening meal, discuss the day's events, and plan for the next day. Flower prepared the evening meal. She enjoyed surprising the men.

The campsite was taking on its spring decorations. Early rye grass, budding bushes, and multicolored flowers filled the countryside. The coyotes announced their nightly hunt. Clint rubbed his belly. "Another great meal. The rest of the crew should be getting back from Santa Fe."

Ty massaged his neck. "I sure miss them."

The conversation led to recounting the challenges they'd faced. Clint led the discussion. "Pulling that stupid bull out of the mud was tough." He tugged on his ear. "I don't think y'all had pulled a calf before, but we got it done. That late freeze was something—breaking ice ain't no fun."

Ty said, "We lost two calves and a mama cow."

Clint frowned and said, "Most ranchers are happy to have a ninety percent calf crop. I'm proud that we checked the cows every day. You and Flower rounded up those ten cows that wandered off. You picked up fifteen unbranded cows and calves. I'd say we've done pretty well."

Flower suddenly said, "A group of horses is coming down the canyon."

Minutes later, Quanah Parker and a small band of warriors rode into camp. He lifted his hand as a sign of peace. The Indians wore riding leggings and buffalo hide coats and feathers indicating their standing in the tribe. There was no war paint. Their horses were big, muscled-up mares.

Ty, in sign language, invited the group to join them at the fire.

Flower retrieved two buffalo skins from her tent and spread them near the fire. They dismounted and sat. Quanah packed his pipe with tobacco and passed it around. Each man smoked it and exhaled a small cloud of smoke. Quanah spoke, "We've been hunting for buffalo. Found none."

Clint responded and told him of the small herd he and Woody found, but he'd seen none since then.

Flower asked, "Are you hungry?"

Quanah did not answer. Flower retreated to her teepee and returned with a supply of buffalo jerky.

Without comment, the Indian guests ate.

Quanah spoke in Comanche, "Sister, our time of freedom is ending. We'll try to keep ahead of the bluecoats, but

I know they'll eventually catch us. The young men are going to fight to the death. I can't talk them out of it."

Flower answered, "Brother, I fear for my people."

Quanah nodded. "I came to see you. I'm happy you and your young man are doing well."

Flower inquired, "How are my people?"

"The blue coats killed two braves while they were hunting. We've had to move. The strain on the old ones is bad." Quanah stroked his pipe. "I don't think we'll have any rest from the soldiers."

Ty responded, "I know one of the officers. Maybe I can talk to him."

"The soldiers do what Bad Hand tells them. The Kiowas attacked the buffalo hunters at Adobe Walls and killed a few before they gave up the fight. The whites want us on a reservation and to give up our lands."

The group sat in silence. Quanah stood and mounted his horse, and the braves followed.

Flower cried out, "Be safe."

The hunting party rode out of camp. When they were gone, Ty remarked, "I didn't catch every word, but I have a good idea what he was saying."

Clint stated, "I don't know why the army can't leave the Injuns alone."

Flower responded, "It's the white man's way."

Seventy

The Flat Top Mountain Ranch – Spring 1867

The travelers from Santa Fe arrived at the ranch. Flower and Ty were preparing a plot of ground for a vegetable garden. Ty yelled, "Welcome home!"

The party dismounted. Woody pointed to the cowboys herding the horses. "This here is Bo and Al. We've taken them on to work the horses and help with the ranch work." He looked at Ty. "Do you think the new corral will hold the horses?"

"Let's find out."

Bo and Al herded the horses into the walled canyon. Ty closed the gate.

Jack stated, "It's been a rough trip. We've purchased an army tent for the new fellas, and we'll pitch it near the dugout."

The new arrivals and Woody were busy putting up the new tent when Clint rode in. "Is that for your new wife?"

"No it ain't—it's for Bo and Al. They'll be working with us." Woody removed his hat and ran his hand around the headband. "You fellas have to ignore Clint. The old man's mind is failing."

Dinner lasted until dark. Each group had stories to tell. Ty read his father's letter to the group. The northern occupation was brutal. As his father predicted, the southern whites had taken up arms against the former slaves. He filled them in on the hate being spread by the Ku Klux Klan.

Jack read parts of his father's letter to the group, telling about the men coming home, missing arms and legs. As Jack read, his hands trembled.

Woody interrupted, "That war didn't need to happen."

Clint added, "Ain't no winners."

Esmeralda grasped Jack's hand.

Ty stood. "It's time for bed. No more talk of the war."

Seventy-One

❖❖

The Flat Top Mountain Ranch – Late Spring 1867

The winter passed, and ranch work was never-ending. Bo and Al took their turns checking the cattle. Their days were filled with breaking the new horses and work on new corrals. Woody and Clint did their share of the work and occasionally hunted for fresh meat. Jack and Ty spent their time searching for unbranded strays. Their herd increased throughout the spring. Also, they'd rounded up ten more mustangs. Esmeralda and Flower worked on their new vegetable garden and making clothes for the men and themselves.

In late spring, O'Brien rode into camp followed by two Conestoga wagons loaded with the supplies Jack had ordered. O'Brien's arrival was cause for celebration and exchange of news.

O'Brien stated, "There's a flood of settlers heading west. The Army has been ordered to escort the pilgrims. In the early spring, Kiowas attacked a group and killed half of the travelers. The Army has been chasing them around up by the

Canadian River like a dog chasing its tail. I've heard that the Army is sending more troops and a new colonel. The new fella's name is Mackenzie."

Jack said, "I've heard of him. He was a general during the war and is a West Point grad. The men who served with him thought well of him. He's not as flashy as some, but he gets the job done without getting his troops killed."

Ty added, "One of his officers served with me at Vicksburg. He's a good man."

Seventy-Two

The Flat Top Mountain Ranch – 1867 to 1873

The partners, their wives, and the cowboys discussed each step of the ranch's growth. Every morning the crew ate breakfast together and planned their day. The land on the west side of the ranch was the beginning of the staked plains. The partners filed and received homestead rights to another six sections of land. Each section was a square mile—six hundred and forty acres.

Winters varied from severe to mild. Ty asked Clint, "Why are the winters so unpredictable?"

"Damned if I know. Been out here twenty-five years, and each year's different"

New pastures meant new fences, and the work never ended. Spring was spent gathering cows, branding calves, and castrating young bulls.

Bo and Al alternated making the trip to Santa Fe. One year, Al brought back a new bride. Upon arriving home with the new couple, Esmeralda beamed at the two old cowboys. "Next year, one of you should come to Santa Fe."

Clint looked at Woody. "Take him."

The ranch's herd grew to one thousand cows and fifty bulls. A horse-breeding program was started. Ty and Jack's mares were retired and turned out with the other breeders. The partners, with Flower's help, purchased stud horses from the Comanches. The offspring of the muscular mares and the swift Indian ponies were excellent horses for the rough country. Each year, the animals to be sold were driven to Santa Fe. The partners spent every dollar of profit improving the ranch.

The westward migration brought a steady stream of settlers to New Mexico and the high plains of Texas. Their trip west was not without peril. Many tribes had been moved to reservations. Quanah Parker's tribe and several bands of Comanche and Kiowas continued to evade the Army.

Mrs. Morales timed her visits to the ranch when each of the children were born. Ty was the proud father of a boy and a girl. Jack's two boys started riding broomsticks around the ranch as soon as they could walk. Ty's girl was born a month after Jack's first son. The other two boys were born two weeks apart.

In the spring of 1874, Clint announced at dinner, "Spring is going to lead into summer before you know it. It's time to cut out the yearling calves and cows that need to be sold. Heard tell that the Army is paying top dollar. This year I think we should take the cows and broke horses to Fort Worth."

The group formulated a plan. Clint, Bo, Al, and Ty would drive the cattle to market. Flower spoke up. "You're going through Comanche country. I'm coming."

The men looked at each other. Clint remarked, "No argument from me."

Esmeralda, Jack, and Woody would stay home and watch the cows.

The day arrived for the group to leave for Fort Worth. Preparation included cutting out ten of the new horses. The cowboys had gathered the cows to be sold on the flat plains. They planned to follow the valley and head due east from Blanco Canyon. Woody, Esmeralda, and Jack joined the group as they started.

Bo remarked, "Them half-broke horses will be ridden by Al and me."

Clint said in a loud voice, "I was riding broncs before you were born."

Ty said, "That's the problem. You're riding point. Flower and I will ride drag."

Clint shook his head and spurred his horse. The herd moved off. After the first mile, Jack motioned to Woody and

Esmeralda. He waved at Ty and said, "Good luck. We'll see you in a month or so."

Flower waved to Esmeralda.

Seventy-Three

The Texas High Plains – Spring 1874

The first hundred miles passed without incident. One night at camp, Flower stated, "My people have left Blanco Canyon. I think the Army found their camp."

Midway through the trip, Clint called a halt. "There's a box canyon half a mile north of here. We're gonna have to get the animals bedded down."

Ty asked, "Why?"

Clint pointed to the south. "See that there cloud? It's moving this way."

Flower nodded. "Let's get moving."

Clint led the cattle to a rough cut in the plains. "This will have to do. Everybody hobble your horses, unload the supplies, and dig a ditch behind the supplies. Let's get a move-on."

With their horses hobbled, the group dug. The wind picked up, storm clouds covered the horizon, and streaks of lightning lit up the sky. In front of the rapidly moving maelstrom, a brown mass of sand was being pushed ahead of the storm.

Clint yelled, "Take your dew rags, wet them, and cover your face. Everyone down in the ditch!"

The howling wind tore at their faces. Grains of sand hit bare skin like a thousand needles. The group huddled together. Their horses turned their backs to the assault. Next, a torrent of rain flooded the improvised ditch.

As quickly as the storm arrived, it dissipated. Clint stood. "It's clear, let's go see to the cows."

They caught and saddled their horses. Clint rode to a small rise and surveyed the scattered animals. "Bo, come with me." Motioning to Ty, Flower, and Al, he said, "Y'all circle west and push the cows to our campsite."

The group spent the rest of the day gathering the scattered animals. Clint explained to the travelers, "We'll keep the cows and horses boxed up tonight. It looks like two horses and five cows are missing. We'll keep watch tonight and move out at first light."

Ty and Flower spread their bedrolls. Ty commented, "I've never seen a storm like that before."

Flower said, "My people call it the devil wind."

Seventy-Four

The Texas High Plains – Spring 1874

The travelers made steady progress. Clint estimated they'd be in Fort Worth within a week. The group set up their camp. During the day's travel, Flower had killed two rabbits and was busy preparing the evening meal.

A squad of soldiers rode into camp. A young lieutenant led the group. "Howdy folks. I see you're herding cattle and it looks like you've got some extra horses. Are they for sale?"

Ty stood. "They are."

"I want to talk to the person in charge."

Clint frowned and pointed at Ty. "He's the man."

Ty continued, "We're taking the cows and extra horses to Fort Worth to sell them."

The lieutenant surveyed the group. "Is that Injun girl with you?"

Rage filled his face. "Yes."

"Maybe we'll camp near you, and the men can have some fun with her."

Ty sprang at the officer and hauled him out of his saddle and drew his revolver. The cowboys and Clint drew their weapons and covered the troopers. Ty growled, "Any more comments like that and I'll blow your brains out."

The officer yelled, "I'm an officer, you can't talk to me like that!" He looked at his troopers. "Sergeant, arrest these people."

The sergeant didn't move and kept his hands raised. "Sir. They got the drop on us."

Ty shouted, "Lieutenant, you might kill us all, but you'll be the first to die."

The sergeant spoke, "Sir. We'd better leave these people alone."

Clint cranked a cartridge into the chamber. "We've got you covered, you'd better git."

Ty motioned for the officer to get back on his horse. "Leave."

His face contorted in anger, the lieutenant ordered his men to follow him. The troop trotted out of camp.

Clint remarked, "I do believe you'd have killed him."

The anger drained from his face, and Ty shook his head. "I almost did."

Flower led him to their bedrolls.

The next day, three soldiers caught up with the herd. Lieutenant Johnson rode in front of two black troopers. Johnson approached Ty. "Can I talk to you?"

Ty looked surprised. "Of course."

Johnson continued, "I've come to apologize to you. The sergeant told me what happened. That lieutenant has been sent home—he's been discharged. Colonel Mackenzie hopes you'll bring your cows and horses to the fort. The army wants to purchase them."

"Sir, I overacted."

Johnson dismounted and motioned Ty to walk with him. "No, you didn't. I want to make amends."

Clint, Bo, Al, and Flower halted the cows and horses, and once settled, they joined Ty and Johnson.

"Introduce me to your wife and these cowboys traveling with you."

They walked back to his companions. "Flower, this is Major Johnson."

Johnson corrected him, saying, "Lieutenant," and tipped his hat.

Flower extended her hand. "He's told me about you. You'll always be welcome in our lodge."

Johnson introduced himself to Clint, Al, and Bo. He added, "The Army's reactivated Fort Belknap. We're in desperate need of beef and remounts."

Clint answered, "If you can come up with ten dollars a head for the cows and two hundred for each horse, we'll be glad to sell them to the army."

Johnson knitted his brow and looked at Ty. "I thought you owned these cows?"

Ty laughed and said, "I do, but Clint is our foreman. What he says goes."

Johnson thought for a moment and said, "Okay, we have a deal." Looking at Clint, he asked, "Do you know how to get to Fort Belknap?"

"Not sure."

"It's north of here about a day's ride. Pushing cattle, it'll probably take two days. If it's alright with you, I'll guide you."

Ty answered, "Good idea."

Johnson mounted his horse. "When we get to the fort, we'll get a good count and settle up. After the business is over, maybe you could join the officers for dinner."

Ty answered, "Our pleasure."

Johnson spurred his horse and rode over to the troopers. As soon he was out of hearing range, Clint remarked, "I don't want to eat with no blue bellies."

Ty chuckled and said, "Maybe there's a single pilgrim woman at the fort."

Clint growled, "We'll rest the stock tonight and move out at first light."

Seventy-Five

Fort Belknap – Spring 1874

Fort Belknap was built in north-central Texas on the frontier to protect and encourage immigration. After the Civil War ended, the purpose of the fort changed. Initially constructed by the 6th Cavalry, the fort was expanded after the Civil War and became the home of the 4th Cavalry. Additional units assigned to the fort were part of the 10th Calvary, a detachment from the 24th Infantry Regiment, better known as Buffalo Soldiers, and twenty Tonkawa scouts.

On arrival at the fort, the cattle and horses were herded into a large pen. When the gate was closed, Clint remarked, "The soldier boys are planning something big. The last time I was here, there were about a hundred soldiers. Their job was to escort wagon trains and protect the settlers on the frontier."

Flower's face contorted as she spoke. "The soldiers have hired those Tonkawa to track my people."

Ty asked, "How do you know that?"

She responded, "They have been our enemy for as long as the old ones can remember. Now that they have a treaty, they lick the soldier's boots."

"Let's ride into the fort and see if we can sell our stock and get out of here."

Flat plains gave way to rolling prairie, and a copse of maple trees extended to a streambed where several cottonwood trees once stood, but all that remained were stumps. The headquarters building was a two-story sandstone building with a covered porch. Newly constructed single-story barracks bracketed the headquarters forming a quadrangle, and the American flag waved proudly in a gentle breeze from a flagpole in the center of the parade grounds. The travelers tied their horses to a hitching post. Lieutenant Johnson dismissed the troopers. Clint remarked to the soldiers, "Thanks for the help, men. If you get tired of army life, look me up."

Johnson mounted the porch and motioned the group to follow him. "Wait here for a minute while I talk to Colonel Mackenzie."

Ty and Clint were ushered into the headquarters of Colonel Ranald S. Mackenzie. He remained seated as the group entered the office. The colonel sat erect in his chair. His neatly trimmed hair and mustache completed his image of a West Point educated officer. Johnson introduced the men to the colonel. Mackenzie sat with his hands clasped.

"The lieutenant tells me you have cattle and horses for sale." His New York accent was unmistakable.

Ty answered, "That's correct."

"He informs me the price is ten dollars a cow and two hundred dollars a horse."

"Yes."

"That's an extraordinary price for those animals."

Ty's anger roiled. "You knew the price before we came into your office. That's the price, take it or leave it."

Mackenzie glared at Ty.

Ty motioned to Clint, and the men turned and headed for the door.

Mackenzie fumed, "We need the animals. Our mission is vital to the security of the settlers heading west. Your government expects its citizens to make sacrifices for the greater good."

Clint turned on his heel. "The man told you the price. Do you want the stock or not?"

"This is highway robbery. But we have no other recourse. I'll pay you your blood money."

Ty wheeled around. "You go to hell." He spun around and opened the door, allowing Clint to exit. Ty slammed the door.

As the party mounted their horses, Lieutenant Johnson exited the office. "Ty, please wait a minute."

"Did I overreact?"

Johnson shook his head. "Sometimes the colonel can be a bit of an ass. I'm authorized to finalize the count and pay you your price."

It didn't take long to verify the count. Johnson went with Ty to the disbursing officer, filled out the army paperwork, and paid Ty.

The disbursing officer, second Lieutenant Knock, slid the bill of sale toward Clint, who motioned Ty to sign. Knock asked, "Can you read?"

Johnson glared at Knock. "You're an idiot. Mr. Jones is better educated than you." He placed his hand on Ty's shoulder. "Please review the documents and see if it agrees with our deal. If it meets with your approval, sign the bill of sale."

Ty signed the bill of sale, turned, and headed out of the office. Johnson caught up with him. Ty extended his hand to Johnson. "Sir, you're a gentleman. I have no desire to spend time with Mackenzie and his other officers."

"I understand. Have a safe trip."

Clint knew a shortcut to the ranch and led the way. As evening approached, he called a halt. Flower prepared a meal of rabbit with fresh scallions and cactus ears. As they sat around the campfire after dinner, drinking coffee, Clint commented, "The Yankee soldiers are preparing for a major battle."

Flower frowned. "They'll be hunting my people."

Clint stated, "Now that the tribes have been dang near destroyed by fever, I suppose the colonel will think he's won a brilliant victory."

Ty sipped his cooling coffee. "The Comanches are some of the best horsemen and fighters I've ever seen."

Clint responded, "That's not what's gonna win the battle—scarce buffalo and white man's germs will kill off the Comanche."

Flower said with a sad smile, "You're right. I've seen this coming for a while."

The next day, after a quick breakfast, the group rode toward home, and even the horses seemed eager to return to familiar pastures.

Seventy-Six

The Flat Top Mountain Ranch – Spring 1874

The group crested a hill. In the distance, the Flat Top Mountain dominated the landscape. Clint stated, "Another two hours, and we'll be home."

They paused by a stream so the horses could drink and graze. Around a bend in the stream, a group of Comanches appeared. Quanah Parker rode at the front. Flower walked toward her brother. Quanah dismounted, and the braves remained on their horses. After a short conversation, Quanah remounted his horse, lifted his hand to Ty and the cowboys, and urged his horse into a trot and bypassed Flower's traveling companions.

Her brow was knit. She cast a sad glance at the retreating Indians. Ty asked, "What's the matter?"

"I have to sit awhile."

Clint said, "Let's pull off our saddles and rest."

The horses were hobbled and grazed along the bank of the stream.

Flower began, "I'm afraid many people are going to be slaughtered. Quanah is creating a false trail for the soldiers to follow. He has relocated his village. The Kiowas and other Comanches are headed to Palo Duro for the winter. Quanah tried to talk them out of going to the canyon because he believes the Army scouts know its location."

Clint reflected, "This has been building up for a lot of years. I can't believe there isn't some way to settle this peacefully."

The group arrived at the Flat Top Mountain Ranch. As they unsaddled their horses, Jack, Esmeralda, and Woody came out to meet them.

Jack asked, "How was the trip?"

Ty answered, "We traded with the Army at Fort Belknap. We got a good price for the animals. Let's go sit down in my house. I want to fill you in."

The group assembled in the combination living room/kitchen. Ty started by describing their meeting with Mackenzie.

Clint filled in details of the preparation the military was making. "They're determined to force Indians onto the reservation."

Ty told of his conversation with Johnson.

Jack commented, "That doesn't seem right."

Clint remarked, "Right has nothing to do with it."

Esmeralda stated, "Why don't we clean up and meet at our house for supper."

All nodded agreement.

Seventy-Seven

The Flat Top Mountain Ranch – August 1874

At the start of each day, everyone ate breakfast together in Jack's cabin. The cabin was a basic design, with several bedrooms opening onto a large dining room/kitchen that served as the gathering place. Plans for the day were discussed, and the status of the livestock evaluated. The breeding season was ending.

Clint stated, "It's time to move the bulls to a separate pasture."

They had decided that after a cow had her first calf, she would be added into the ranch's breeding cycle. Sales depended on what their biggest customer, the U.S. Government, wanted. Reservations in the Oklahoma territory and New Mexico needed a steady supply of beef for the imprisoned Indians.

The ranch had been raided several times by comancheros and Kiowas, and horses and cows were stolen. Each time, the raiders learned that stealing from the Flat Top Mountain

Ranch was not a good idea. Each theft was rewarded with swift retribution. On one occasion it took Clint, Ty, and the cowboys two months to catch up with the culprits. Besides recovering the stolen stock, they confiscated the raiders' horses—the Army always needed new mounts.

The plan was settled, and the ranch crew disbursed to do the day's work. Ty, Clint, and two cowboys went out to saddle their horses and round up the bulls and move them. Jack and Woody were tasked with inspecting the yearling calves and the mother cows.

They were mounted when a troop of soldiers rode into the ranch headquarters. Leading the troops was Lieutenant Johnson. He reined up in front of the group.

Johnson greeted them. "How have you been getting on?"

Ty responded, "Fine, sir. Why do you ask?"

"We are planning to gather the remaining Indians and take them to the reservation. We've been chasing them for two years, and they've slipped through our fingers. Washington is pressuring the Army. They want the Indians settled on the reservation. The colonel knows Flower is Quanah's sister, and he thinks she probably knows their hideouts."

Flower came out of the cabin, having overheard the conversation. Before she could speak, Ty held up his hand. "Lieutenant Johnson, we don't know where they're camped. We wouldn't tell you if we did."

The lieutenant saw that Ty was getting agitated. "Ty, I was ordered to ask you. I told the colonel what your answer would be, but I had my orders."

Ty responded, "I'm not going to help the Army slaughter more Indians."

"I hope this can be accomplished with a minimum of casualties."

Ty exhaled. "I know you're following orders."

Johnson answered, "I know you don't think much of Colonel Mackenzie. He's a fine officer and takes no pleasure in killing."

Ty nodded and said, "I hope you're correct."

After the troopers had ridden away, Flower said, "Do you think all my people will be killed?"

"Lieutenant Johnson is a good man. He takes no pleasure in killing."

Seventy-Eight

Palo Duro Canyon – September 1874

Johnson caught up with the rest of the force. Their scouts had located the Indian encampment at the head of the Palo Duro Canyon. Mackenzie motioned Johnson to ride with him. "What did you find out from the rancher?"

"Nothing, sir. They will not help us. They're afraid that we'll slaughter the Indians."

"Didn't you tell them that was not our plan?"

"Yes, sir. They're skeptical."

"No matter. Return to your squad. We'll march to the path the scouts found down the escarpment. Be prepared to move at first light."

Johnson saluted and returned to his men. "We'll ride to the head of the trail and rest until first light. There's to be no fires, smoking or noise. It's important to maintain silence and discipline. There will be no shooting until I tell you. Is that understood?"

The men all nodded.

The column arrived at the trailhead and unsaddled and hobbled their horses. Guards took their positions, and each trooper ate beef jerky and biscuits from his saddlebag. They washed down dinner with water. Some men slept, while others rested, too anxious about the upcoming battle to sleep.

The horizon cast a gray glow as preparations were made for the descent down the steep trail. Mackenzie sent runners to each company commander to join him. "We're going to have to lead our horses down the trail. I plan to surprise the Indians before they're fully awake. There's been enough killing in this war, and it's time to get this last bunch of holdouts to the reservation in Oklahoma territory. Lieutenant Johnson, your company will be first. The balance of the regiment will follow by companies. There is to be no firing until I order it."

Johnson returned to his troopers. "We're going to lead our horses single file down the trail. There will be no talking. Double-check the canvas wrapping on your horse's hooves and follow your sergeant. Maintain a horse length separation."

Johnson headed for the start of the trail. An Indian guide led the way. Johnson followed. The trail was steep and strewn with loose rocks, and mesquite thorns tore at the soldiers' uniforms. Discipline was maintained. The troopers had been chasing the Comanches and Kiowas for many years. This was their opportunity to end this war. Thousands of Indians had been settled on reservation land. The men knew this group included some of the remaining holdouts.

The guide edged down the trail. Johnson raised his hand and pointed to a solitary sentry at the bottom of the trail. The guard was asleep. Johnson motioned for a trooper to neutralize the sleeping Indian.

The troopers spread out around the sleeping village. The sun was creeping down the canyon walls.

Mackenzie followed the men down the trail. At the bottom, he directed each troop of cavalry to the place he wanted them. They blocked the exit up the escarpment. Next, he instructed Johnson to mount his troopers and find the pony herd. "When you find the ponies, fire a shot. I've ordered the men to not target any Indians unless they are in danger. Let's hope we can scatter the ponies and chase the tribe down the canyon."

The shot reverberated throughout the canyon. Flaps on teepees exploded open, and the warriors grabbed what weapons they could, while women and children ran away. The warriors scrambled for cover and tried to mount a defense. Mackenzie ordered his soldiers to shoot to kill only if it was necessary to prevent injury to himself or another soldier.

With nowhere to run and no horses to flee on, the warriors formed a rearguard behind the women and children. The Indians fled, and some attackers followed at a safe distance. Mackenzie ordered his remaining troopers to burn the village and all the provisions for the upcoming winter. The heat of the fire forced the soldiers to retreat. Black smoke rose from the encampment. This battle was over.

The Comanche and Kiowa chiefs conferred, and they agreed. "We have no other place to run. We must start walking to the reservation."

Johnson and his men chased the pony herd down the canyon, away from the frustrated braves. His guides knew where to take the horses—Tule Creek. The twenty-mile ride assured that the Indians had no transportation. At a box canyon in the creek, the horses were forced into a circle. Johnson thought, *The best way to end this war is to destroy the enemy's means of transportation.*

After the horses settled down, he ordered the troopers to kill all the horses. Shots rang out, and the screeches of stricken animals brought chills to the troopers, but they followed their orders. The slaughter ended, and the last horse whined and dropped to the ground. Johnson had his soldiers form into a line. "Men, I know this was not what you expected, but the loss of these horses ends the war. The only option the Indians have is to walk to the reservation."

Seventy-Nine

The Flat Top Mountain Ranch – September 1874

Johnson led the troopers back toward Palo Duro Canyon. As they approached the canyon, they could see clouds of smoke. When they caught up with the rest of the soldiers, Johnson reported the slaughter of the Indian ponies. Mackenzie stated, "We're going to follow the Indians back to the reservation. You have another mission." He explained what he wanted. Johnson led his troopers back up the trail and headed for the Flat Top Mountain Ranch.

Johnson and his troopers arrived at the ranch headquarters as the sun was setting. Ty, Jack, their wives, and the cowboys sat in silence as the soldiers approached. Johnson dismounted, "We chased the tribes out of the Palo Duro, and they're walking to the reservation."

Flower asked, "How many did you kill?"

"One man." He bowed his head, "That's one more than we wanted to kill, but it was unavoidable."

"Why are they walking?"

"We killed all their horses."

Sadness filled Flower's face. "My people can't fight the army without their ponies."

Johnson addressed the group, "The army needs to purchase as many cattle as you can spare. We've destroyed their supplies, and we are obliged to see to their welfare."

Clint remarked, "We'll gather the excess cows and steers in the morning." Ty and Jack nodded their agreement.

Ty offered, "Why don't you and your men camp here tonight. We'll rustle up some food."

Johnson smiled and said, "We'll take you up on that."

As they ate, Johnson described the battle at Palo Duro. He looked at Flower. "Quanah and his group were not at Palo Duro. There's been a troop of scouts and soldiers running around in circles trying to catch him."

Ty remarked, "You're chasing the best of the best. Maybe it's lucky you didn't catch him. When he's ready, he'll make peace."

The yearling calves were pastured on the plains above the canyon. Clint's, Ty's, and the cowboys' task was to separate the fatter calves. Sorting took most of the morning. When the job was complete, they drove the calves to the pens near the headquarters.

Woody and Jack, with two cowboys, rode through the cows. After selecting the animals to be sold, they herded them to the stockade where the yearling calves waited.

Clint greeted Woody. "Did you sort out that old one eyed broken-horned rascal that almost ran me down?"

"No! She was waiting for you. Didn't want to spoil your fun."

The cavalry troop was saddled and waiting. Ty asked, "Which way?"

Johnson responded, "We can head northeast. I've sent three men to locate the colonel. He'll decide where to meet."

Flower and Esmeralda spent the morning preparing food for the trip and loading two mules for the journey.

As the partners approached the headquarters, they saw that Flower was sitting on her horse. Jack remarked, "It looks like your wife is coming."

Ty sighed, "She told me she was coming."

That night the troopers and cattlemen camped by the banks of a tributary of the Red River. Clint assigned night herd duties. They strung rope lines between cottonwood trees and unsaddled the horses and gave them grain. Woody and Flower prepared the evening meal. The troopers had their own trail rations.

At sunup, the group was ready to move. Progress was steady. The troopers rode in a flanking position. During their midday rest, the dispatched soldiers returned. The corporal leading the patrol rode into camp, stepped down from his horse, and saluted his company commander. "The colonel is camped near Adobe Walls, thirty miles north of here. He plans to rest the troopers. Patrols are following the Indians."

"Good job, Corporal. Relax and have a bite to eat, and we'll head out when you're ready."

The party packed up and headed out. Lieutenant Johnson and the corporal rode in front of the party.

Ty and Jack shared looks. Ty remarked, "Adobe Walls, that's where we met."

"Yup, how many years ago was that?"

"Damned if I know."

They laughed as they rode to catch up with the herd.

Eighty

Adobe Walls – October 1874

It took the party two days to meet up with Mackenzie. The troopers had erected tents and made cooking circles. The soldiers had not rested since the campaign started two months earlier. The Kiowas and Comanches camped a mile away in a dry playa lake. Troopers were posted near their encampment.

Lieutenant Johnson and his company rode into the army camp. He called a halt and turned to his sergeant. "See to the men—I'm going to report to the colonel."

"Excellent, sir," The sergeant said and then bellowed, "Dismount and unsaddle your horses, take them to water, and turn them out to pasture."

Mackenzie exited his tent as Johnson dismounted and saluted. "Colonel, we've secured fifty head of cattle from the Flat Top Mountain Ranch."

Mackenzie acknowledged, "Very good." He added, "I wasn't sure the ranchers would help us. Go get something to eat and rest up. I'm going to talk with the ranchers and ride over to the Indian encampment and invite the chiefs to our camp."

Johnson saluted and led his horse to his company's bivouac area.

Colonel Mackenzie rode to meet the ranchers. Ty and Jack separated from the group. Mackenzie touched his hat. "Thank you for delivering the cows. I'll have a pay voucher drawn up to cover the cost of the animals and your time."

Jack answered, "We'll wait here for payment and then head back to our place."

"Gentlemen, please join me for a campfire meal. I've sent a man to ask Mananti, chief of the Kiowas, and O-he-ma-ta, one of the Comanche chiefs, to join us." Looking at Ty, he said, "I see your wife accompanied you. Will you ask her to join us?"

Ty and Jack conferred in a whisper. Ty answered, "I will."

"Excellent. Lieutenant Johnson will be joining us. After you get your cattle settled, meet me at my tent."

Ty, Jack, Clint, and Flower rode into the cavalry encampment. Mackenzie's tent was easy to recognize as it was the largest. In front were mounted an American flag and the regimental colors. Several canvas camp tables were aligned, and fold-down canvas chairs were distributed around the table. Mackenzie stepped out of his tent as the ranchers approached. "Welcome, I'm happy you could make it."

Lieutenant Johnson stood at his side. Ty and Jack led their small contingent. Ty spoke, "I'm happy that your battle with the Comanches and Kiowas didn't result in a slaughter."

Mackenzie smiled and said, "And so am I. Mr. Johnson has told me about you. We've both seen enough killing to last a lifetime."

Ty looked at Flower. "Maybe we can live in peace."

Mackenzie replied, "I hope so."

Two troopers escorted the Comanche and Kiowa chiefs to the colonel's tent. The Indian leaders were riding Army horses. Colonel Mackenzie motioned for them to dismount and join the group. He turned toward the troopers, "Return to your outfit and be ready to escort the chiefs back to their camp."

O-he-ma-ta acknowledged Flower with a nod. The Kiowa chief, Mananti, stood in silence. Mackenzie looked relieved. "I didn't know if you'd accept my invitation."

O-he-ma-ta answered, "What choice do I have?"

Mackenzie's face showed no emotion. "Probably none. This war is over. There's a government agent at the reservation who will show you the land your tribes are being given."

Mananti spoke in Spanish, "You say you're giving us land. Don't insult me. This was all our land. You've defeated most of my people, and some still fight. My tribe will do what we have to do. We want to live in peace."

Ty served as an interpreter. When he'd finished the translation, he asked, "Do you want to respond?"

"We have a treaty . . . "

O-he-ma-ta raised his hand and spoke in English. "No more talk of treaties. The whites never keep their word. You've killed our horses and destroyed our food. The cattle from my friend's ranch will help us survive until we arrive at the reservation." He looked at Mananti and in sign language said, "I don't see any reason to fight with Bad Hand. The cattle will help our people survive." O-he-ma-ta acknowledged with a nod. Looking at Mackenzie, he said, "We have no desire to sit with you. The cattle are welcome. Is it possible to let us have some horses to herd the cattle?"

"No. My troopers will drive the cattle. When you need cows, you tell them, and they will bring you as many as you need."

The two chiefs turned and walked back to their camp.

Mackenzie stood, watching the chief's retreat. He addressed Flower. "Will you tell your brother that I'll guarantee his safety if he returns to the reservation?"

Flower answered, "No." She turned and headed toward her horse. Ty, Jack, and Clint followed her.

Lieutenant Johnson caught up with Ty and Jack. "Let's settle up with the disbursing officer, Lieutenant Knock."

Ty smiled. "Sure, time for some fun."

Without comment, Knock handed the bill of sale to Ty. The partners spent a minute reading the document, signed it, and returned it to the stone-faced disbursing officer.

Johnson looked at Ty and Jack. "Is that satisfactory?"

Ty answered, "It looks okay. If it isn't, I'll be back and show Mr. Knock how we castrate. Maybe my brother-in-law, Quanah, can help me."

Knock's face turned pale.

Eighty-One

The Indian Wars

The war on the south plains was substantially over, but other skirmishes and raids by groups of disaffected braves continued during the balance of the nineteenth century. The tribes that settled on the reservations remained peaceful.

The Indian wars continued in other areas of the country. At the Little Big Horn, Custer and the 7th Cavalry were destroyed by an overwhelming force of Indians equipped with repeating rifles, while the troopers fought with single-shot arms left over from the Civil War. Quanah, on hearing the news, commented, "Yellow hair has paid for the slaughtering of the Cheyenne people at Washita." Quanah's face showed the pain he felt in his response. "I'm afraid that one victory will not chase the white men from our land. The people's journey to the reservation will be a trail of tears."

Mackenzie was ordered to the Apache lands in Arizona and New Mexico. He subdued the Apaches by continually chasing them from one hideout to the next. The Apaches' final refuge was in the Mexican mountains. A concerted effort of soldiers from both countries drove the Apaches to the reservation.

An uprising by the Nez Perce was ended by the rumor that Bad Hand was coming.

Mackenzie succeeded at ending the Indian Wars. He retired from the Army with the rank of brigadier general. He died in 1889 at age 48. During his career, he was overshadowed by George A. Custer. Mackenzie was a bitter man. He could not understand how a leader who got his men killed could be lionized.

Eighty-Two

The Flat Top Mountain Ranch – Peace and Growth

After the Palo Duro Battle, Sean O'Brien gave up his transport business and opened a dry goods store. The trading post was located ten miles north of the Flat Top Mountain Ranch. He named his store Quitaque, which in Indian language translates to "end of the trail." Another translation of Quitaque says it means piles of horse crap. When this was pointed out to O'Brien, he retorted, "No self-respecting Scot would live in a place named after English whiskey."

When Jack's father passed away, he and Esmeralda traveled to Grahamsville, NY. His brothers were enthralled with Esmeralda. Jack's brother, Luke, had taken a wife. One evening at supper, the conversation came around to settling the family business. Jack was the first to speak. "Y'all don't owe me nothing. Without Daddy's help, I could not have started my ranch."

Mike was next to talk. "I've been thinking. If you and Esmeralda can put up with me, I'd like to come with you to Texas."

Jack's face lit up. "That would be great. My partner and I have been talking about breaking out some of our flat pasture and planting wheat. You're a better farmer than I could ever hope to be."

Luke interrupted, "With your share of Dad's estate, you won't be going to Texas empty-handed."

Esmeralda beamed at Mike, "I can't wait for you to meet my cousin."

Jack broke down in laughter.

Mike asked, "What's so funny?"

Esmeralda jabbed Jack in the ribs.

Containing himself, Jack answered, "Nothing. Our two top hands will be glad to meet you."

Esmeralda responded with another jab.

The Flat Top Mountain Ranch expanded onto the Llano Estacado (the staked plains). The ranch family grew, with both Flower and Esmeralda giving birth to more children. Clint and Woody remained bachelors. The partners built onto their homes and family members visited.

On one of Mr. Boudreaux's visits, there was an additional visitor. Quanah stopped at the ranch with twelve of his young warriors. When they rode in, Flower greeted the Comanches and introduced Ty's father. Mr. Boudreaux and Quanah took turns holding Ty and Flower's children. Quanah commented, "They look like Topsannah."

Mr. Boudreaux, after a hearty laugh, commented, "That's a good thing."

Quanah was passing through to go on a buffalo hunt with Charles Goodnight. Quanah spent time discussing the events that led to the defeat of the Comanches. The ranch crew sat in rapt silence. Mr. Boudreaux said, "That's a remarkable story. You don't hold a grudge?"

Quanah responded, "Hate got many killed. We have to look toward the future."

Ty nodded and Mr. Boudreaux's face lit up as he thought, *My happy boy is back. No more anger.*

Acknowledgments

Without my wife, my friend, and my editor, Denise, writing would be impossible. She reads my first draft and has the patience and red pens.

Thank you to my three sons—James, Bernard, and Patrick—who never interrupt when I repeat a story for the hundredth time.

To my grandchildren—Matthew, James III, Brendan, and Janey: "They'll learn much more than I'll ever know." (Taken from the lyrics of "What a Wonderful World.")

Thanks also to the Witness Writers Group and our intrepid leader, Carol Bell.

Thanks to my cousin, Gary Coltart. He reads my first drafts and always is supportive.

And last, thanks to the team at Aloha Publishing—Maryanna Young and Jennifer Regner—two women who are a joy to work with.

.

About the Author

James E. Doucette was raised in Bedford Stuyvesant, Brooklyn, New York. He joined the U.S. Navy in 1957 and completed high school and college at night. He worked for several telecommunications companies until 1983. In 1984, he founded Cablevision of Texas, constructed or purchased over four hundred cable television systems, and purchased a telephone installation company and a home security service.

In 1990, he purchased the First National Bank of Lockney and during the next eight years, added four additional banks. He began selling his businesses in 1998 and retired in 1999.

Jim and his wife Denise live on a ranch in Floyd County, Texas. At the beginning of 2019, they sold the last of their cows. Today, they rent the grazing rights to local cattlemen. They have been blessed with three sons, a daughter recently deceased, and four grandchildren. Jim wrote his first book, *The Not So Great American Novel*, a memoir, in 2015. His other published books are *Stealing Fire*, which was republished as *Russia's Biggest Hack*, and *The Last Assassination*. He also contributed to the writing of *Witnesses to the Crucifixion:*

Stories of Redemption and the Healing Power of Jesus, authored by Ricky Carstensen.

The Works of
James E. Doucette

Jim started writing as therapy a number of years ago. His first book was *The Not So Great American Novel*, which was a memoir of his life in business.

That title was an attempt at humor—and the literary majors in his writing group immediately jumped on this with no humor whatsoever, because **a biography is not a novel**. Okay, then.

His first two novels, *Stealing Fire* (which was republished as *Russia's Biggest Hack*) and *The Last Assassination*, are historical fiction. Many of the fictitious events he invented for these novels came true—so he made fake news before anyone heard of it.

The Flat Top Mountain Ranch: The Beginning is also historical fiction but it's doubtful the real world will imitate his imagination in this one.

His next book will take you back to the Flat Top Mountain Ranch in the contemporary world. The protagonists end up in West Texas when their worlds in California and New York fall apart. Can these nomads find contentment in their new environment? He'll be exploring this as he writes. Those pesky characters sometimes take him to places he never dreamed of. You'll have to wait and see how it turns out.

If you have any comments about this book or any of his books, please contact Jim via email at james_doucette@ yahoo.com. He promises to answer you.

His books are available on Amazon.com

www.ingramcontent.com/pod-product-compliance
Lightning Source LLC
Chambersburg PA
CBHW021529250626
47154CB00006BA/2041